Nocturne Pondicherry

Ari Gautier is the author of *Carnet secret de Lakshmi*, *Le Thinnai* and *Nocturne Pondichéry*, three French-language books that creatively blend several languages including French, Tamil, Sanskrit, English and Pondicherry Creole.

Nominated for the prestigious French literary award Le Prix du Printemps du livre du forum de Saint Louis, Ari has gained international recognition for his works that provide insight into India's history, the city's multicultural dynamism, the Indian caste system and the impact of French rule in Pondicherry. His first book *Lakshmi's Secret Diary*, translated into English by Sheela Mahadevan, will be published in August by the prestigious Columbia University in the USA. Gautier has currently finished a new collection of short stories that is awaiting publication.

After a few years spent in France, he currently lives in Oslo.

Roopam Singh is a translator and journalist with a special focus in art and culture. Having studied and worked over two decades in India and France, she has brought added value in translation to a fair number of individuals and organizations. She has translated plays, poems, ballets, short stories from French to English and vice versa. *Nocturne Pondicherry* is her first big publication in fiction.

PRAISE FOR THE BOOK

The nocturne is a musical form played at the onset of night, when all the serenading is over and done with; Ari Gautier's tone may be lyrical, expressive and humane, but he pulls no punches in what he writes. With insouciance and huge ambition, Gautier sets static, tourist Pondicherry in motion; in this collection, that place is no longer imprisoned within the limits of the boulevard town. His readers are going to see Pondicherry in altogether different types of light.

Ian H. Magedera, author of *Indian Videshinis, European Women in India*

Transgressors coded with charisma stalk the pages of Ari Gautier's *Nocturne Pondicherry*, and these outliers move with kineticism. The prose is studded with lyricism, which is both thrilling and precise, and in this magnetic literary smackdown, Gautier dares the reader to look away. A triumph.

Diriye Osman, author of *Fairytales for Lost Children*

The stories in this collection are deeply disturbing stories carrying the fragrance and the stench of a land that was entangled in a culture of the colonisers, with lasting memories of vulnerable women surrounded by debauched men, of sensitive men trying to find meaning of their lives, of unfulfilled love and deep longings of exiled women and men for a land that keeps beckoning them.

Ambai, author of *A Red-necked Green Bird*

Ari Gautier's Nocturne Pondicherry is a voyage into the heart of Pondicherry. Beautifully translated from the French original by Roopam Singh, this deeply immersive collection of short stories is exhilarating, extraordinary and exquisitely written. Gautier is an incredibly gifted author whose prose makes us pause, reflect and re-read. The characters so real, calling us back to Pondicherry again and again, luring us until we are intrinsically lost in their lives. If you pick one book this year, make sure it's Nocturne Pondicherry. You're in for a treat because this is short story writing at its very best.

Priya Hein, author of *Riambel*

These are captivating stories full of the music and sights of a distinctive part of India, narrated with love, humour and perception.

Tabish Khair, author of *The Body by the Shore*

Nocturne Pondicherry

Stories

Ari Gautier

Translated from the French original by

Roopam Singh

hachette INDIA

First published in French in 2021 by Editions L'Harmattan, France

This translation first published in India in 2024 by Hachette India
(Registered name: Hachette Book Publishing India Pvt. Ltd)
An Hachette UK Company
www.hachetteindia.com

1

ISBN 978-93-5731-881-5

Hachette Book Publishing India Pvt. Ltd
4th/5th Floors, Corporate Centre,
Plot No. 94, Sector 44, Gurugram 122003, India

Typeset in Adobe Garamond Pro 11.5/17.2
by InoSoft Systems, Noida

Printed and bound in India by
Manipal Technologies Limited

MIX
Paper | Supporting responsible forestry
FSC™ C043100

For Axel and Annika,
two stars shining in my literary sky

Contents

Viji 1

Mani Enna? 19

The Exile 33

Malarvizhi 53

The Golden Cage 63

Marguerite 81

The Postman, the Madman and the Drunk 103

Glossary (Tamil–English) 133

Viji

Taking long strides, Viji quickened her pace. She took the tip of her *dhavani* to wipe the sweat trickling down her neck and forehead. She had just reached the Odiansalai roundabout and quickly glanced at the liquor shop by the corner of the street just before Newton Theatre. The shiny clock on the wall showed 5 p.m. The young girl turned right before heading straight to her neighbourhood. She went past curious onlookers scouting around the cinema hall. There were very few people there, mostly men roaming around, smoking and looking at an enticing poster of a Malayali film. In it, the popular actress Shakeela was sitting on a tiny stool that was barely visible beneath her curves. Her wet *paavadai* was clinging to her elephant-like body, inciting sighs from thousands of men across the country. The pink plastic bucket placed in front of her looked miniscule. She was holding a pot in her right hand, pouring water over her head. In the backdrop, one could see a silhouette of a masculine face watching over. The film looked promising. Viji lowered her head while passing by, avoiding eye contact with those randy men. However, some of them stopped to look at the poster and at her, whispering lasciviously. Disgusted, she quickly walked past them.

She looked up only upon reaching the Sri Ram Hotel. The sun was slowly fading into the horizon behind the rice fields of Ozhukarai. The trees from the botanical garden looked paralysed under the tyranny of the sun god. Looking through the grill, the young woman could see lovers sitting under the trees, looking bored. She stopped for a moment to look at them and sighed as she went on her way, her right foot shaking as her sandal suddenly gave way. Surprising, since she had her sandals repaired only a week ago. She took them off and bent down to pick them up. The ground was still warm. She looked sadly at the tamarind tree behind Subbaiah's statue. As she looked at the skinny silhouette of the old shoemaker, her face lit up. He was chatting with his friend, the rickshaw puller.

'Viji, what do you want me to do with your old sandals? I told you the other day that I won't be able to repair them any more. There is nothing more to be done with them. Why are you so adamant about keeping them? Look at these ones here. If you like them, you can take them. You can pay me later. Bit by bit.'

The old shoemaker caressed his big moustache with fingers blackened by wax. He then took the sandal and turned it around, looking for a way to repair it. He shook his head and gave up. He had held these sandals in his hands many times. But this time around, nothing could be done. As Viji hesitantly looked on, without saying a word, he threw them in the heap of leather waste behind the tamarind tree.

'*Aiyyo, Thatha!*' The young girl felt a surge of desperation. 'Please, this is the last time. Please! I am already late. If I leave without my shoes, how will I manage? You know the devil who lives in my house, don't you? Imagine going home without my shoes! Disaster! Do something! I just need to walk a few metres!'

'My dear, I can't do anything. These sandals will not even last one hundred meters! Listen to me. I can't keep saying the same thing all the time. Stop wasting my time! Take these ones, and you can pay me whenever you can.'

He took a piece of the cloth hanging over his shoulder to wipe his back and went back to talk to the rickshaw puller who, stretched across his vehicle, was nearly falling off to sleep.

Viji glanced from the pile of waste leather pieces to the new shiny sandals lying on a jute cloth in front of the shoemaker. She hesitated. The sandals with yellow straps were shining like gold under the sun as it went down. They would go well the orange *churidar* she had bought for Pongal. If she took them, she would wear them only on special occasions. They were beautiful. She could already see herself walking in them on the Cours Chabrol by the seaside, taking in the fresh air. She would sit down, put her sandals on the rock and dream of faraway lands. The wind would carry her on waves of happiness to shores where millions of shoes could be found under giant coconut trees. The girls in the neighbourhood would be jealous. The sound of the anvil brought her back to reality. The shoemaker had taken her old sandals and finished repairing them. She thanked him with a smile and made her way home feeling lighter.

Vijaya! Victory! One should have given the highest award for sarcasm to her parents, especially to her mother, who chose this glorious name for her firstborn. This was also the name of the Goddess Durga. However, since her birth, the young girl fell prey to defeat.

A few days after her birth, her maternal grandfather, who worked as an electrician at the Régie Dubrayapet, was diagnosed with leprosy. No one knew how he had contracted this shameful disease, but everyone said that the cause of leprosy found its roots in the whereabouts of Sannyasi Thoppu (or Sannyasi Grove). Since his wife died early in life, the only people who could look after him were his daughter and son-in-law. The latter claimed to be a carpenter but was actually a good-for-nothing. No one had ever seen him make a single piece of furniture in his life. Not even a *manakkatai*! Her grandfather lost his job and was chased out of his neighbourhood. He then took refuge in a miserable slum behind the tiny chapel of Saint-Antoine, on the way to Nellitope. In those days, a small community of shepherds was breeding sheep in this area known for its slaughterhouses. The slum had expanded since the construction of a new bus stand next to Anna Theatre and Mass Hotel. The once idyllic setting transformed into an infernal ghetto and a hub of vices. Alcohol, prostitution, gambling, drugs, hooligans, henchmen and lost souls found their bearings in this depraved little island. Most of the people who lived there were servants working in the White Town. Life was atrociously violent. Drunkards with harsh voices spewed vociferous insults that echoed in the four corners of the slum, their bodies assaulted by beatings from neighbours or from the nearby *saarayakadai*. Men and women lived a painful existence in this inferno cursed by God. When evening fell upon the slum, the sun passed on the infamous day to the moon, and the men and women returned, dragging their feet, carrying dirty torn bags of leftovers from the homes of the masters they worked for. The slum was ready to clean its atrocious face and curl up to the people guzzling *saarayam* and *kallu*. Virtue hid itself under the cover of the darkness – a darkness everyone hoped would last forever. At night an animal state brought forth monsters that nobody had the courage to battle. These monsters went from house to house, throwing up their sufferings and their frustrations. In each hut, men opened drawers filled with dirty secrets, of sleazy pleasures and demonic desires. Tired after the day's work, the residents let themselves be asphyxiated by an invisible, villainous and ignominious gas. In the evening, these simple beings turned into vultures, crapulous and procuring, transforming the otherwise peaceful place into a crematorium where living cadavers danced on the ashes of their misery. Trapped in an obscure kingdom, these men and women danced until they fell into a circle of shouts, laughter, sniggers and tears. It was as if they needed all this vulgarity and violence to face the next dawn.

These were the conditions in which Viji's grandfather contracted leprosy and was thrown out of his neighbourhood to take refuge in the slum and become a weed peddler. After his death, Viji's mother had no choice but to follow in her father's footsteps.

'Why are you late?' The slap came before the answer. Viji's right hand was trembling as she covered her face with her left hand. Normally, she would have cried. Torrents of tears would have rolled down her face and neck. But today, she stood like a statue in front of her mother, not wanting to answer or confront her. She was showing a certain detachment and disdain. She was also smiling mysteriously. Her mother frowned, moving on to sit under the banyan tree at the side of the hut. All those who knew her called her the Banyan Tree Lady. There was no need to choose between hashish or weed – the Banyan Tree Lady had enough of both. Since her childhood, Viji knew only this image of her mother, sitting beside the hut and under the huge banyan tree, hidden by the creepers. She spent her days selling weed rolled in newspapers. Once a month, she went for two days to Madurai to get her stash. Viji's alcoholic and unemployed father was just a drunk intoxicated ghost, either in the background or knocked out under the hut. Clarity and good sense had left this man since the beginning of time. His brothers and sisters were too young to understand the abject condition they lived in.

After her shower, Viji took the clothes packed in an old metallic suitcase and stuffed them into a big canvas bag from Ram Silk House. Her entire wardrobe was contained in this disfigured suitcase. She looked at the roof of the hut made of coconut leaves. She then found a familiar spot, and with her right hand pulled out a roll hidden between the leaves and hid it in her upper garment. She went to the tiny toilet that was just a slab covered on all sides by coconut leaves. She did her hair in front of the mirror hanging from a moringa tree. She took a box of Pond's talcum powder from the shelf hanging on a white-washed wall and smeared it on her face and neck. She was about to leave when her mother shouted.

'Have you finished your makeup, you shithead? Do you think you are the queen of Vattalakundu or what? There is no king or prince waiting for you! Hurry up! Your first client will not wait for long! This idiotic auto rickshaw driver is late!'

Client! She had heard this word since she was fifteen years old, and it was now a part of her cursed existence. Client, the hideous monster that emerged only with nightfall. Client, the despicable shadow appearing when the accomplice night enveloped the miserable slum, while the moon left in shame, abandoning the game to hide behind the clouds. Viji was only fifteen when she was put on the altar of sacrifice. The altar was none other than the office of the sub-inspector of police of Odiansalai, who, tired of the dirty money coming from the racket, settled for young and innocent flesh. In this land, the worst criminals were the ones who were supposed to fight crime.

She remembered how on Diwali the sub-inspector's police jeep stopped in front of the banyan tree. It was not the first time. Sankar Mama, as Viji called him, was a regular there. He came two or three times a month. He knew her mother since her pestiferous grandfather's time. On this festival, Sankar reached a little more drunk than usual. His bloodshot eyes nearly popping out of their sockets, reflecting his drunken state. He was wearing a sardonic smile. His fat belly pressed against the banyan tree. His *chillum* was ready. Viji's father lit it and handed it over to him. Sankar Mama closed his eyes and took long drags. The bitter smoke rose up and blended into the smoke of the firecrackers. For a moment, he looked absent, then, as if suddenly remembering something important, he waved to the young woman who was playing in front of the hut. Hesitantly, Viji came closer to the man. She had never liked him, especially since his obscene behaviour towards her. As soon as she came close, he took her in his arms and made her sit on his lap. He kissed her and tickled her with his thick moustache. As she started to object, her mother scolded her. 'It's Sankar Mama. He is kissing you out of love,' she said, smiling with difficulty. As he got ready to leave, Viji's mother unrolled a bundle of money and held out her palm. The policeman refused silently and with his chin gestured towards the young girl. Her mother was neither offended nor surprised. The young girl found her mother's reaction more than surprising. For a long time, she had known that this would happen someday. A few minutes later, her mother asked the young girl to get into the jeep. And they left.

Viji returned at nightfall to the neighbourhood broken out in joy and euphoria. Firecrackers burst everywhere. Stars, rockets and jets lit up the cloudy sky. Cones placed in front of the houses threw their light at the night sky and on Viji's face, who, usually, marvelled at this explosion of colours and sounds. That night, she walked around like the living dead among the firecrackers. Children ran around in the narrow streets, wearing new clothes and screaming in delight. All the houses and huts were illuminated with oil lamps. Her life – thrown into darkness – contrasted with this bursting light. It was in this silence that the young girl's mother washed her blood-stained *dhavani*.

Viji came out of the hut at the sound of Murugan's auto rickshaw. He was the chosen driver to take her to clients in sordid hotels. Murugan was also her bodyguard, go-between, friend and secret lover. Even though he did not admit his love for her, she knew that he loved her, without saying so. He was known to the family since that dark night he brought over a client looking for weed. Murugan had spotted him near the Mass Hotel. Dressed in a *veshti*, the man seemed to be looking for something. He was holding on tight to a big canvas bag against his chest in a strange manner. He had come out of the porch at the back of the hotel into a dark and gloomy lane to the right of the bus stand. It was the hidden exit for clients coming to the cabaret. He had had a drink too many but was not drunk. He looked happy and cocky like most men who came to the cabaret. Murugan knew how to recognize them. He could read it in their eyes; their desire for forbidden things giving them away. They always hesitated a bit while coming out of the hotel and looked around, hunting for a secret sign that would define the rest of the evening. Suspicious-looking men and women moved around the smelly lane looking for their prey.

The man came closer to Murugan and asked him where the closest bar was. The auto-rickshaw driver detected a southern accent – more precisely from Tirunelveli – and judging by his appearance, concluded that he was a villager. He held on to his prey.

The man wanted to drink and have some more fun even though it was late. The old French colony was reminiscent of British culture. The bars closed an hour before midnight. Murugan knew the town like the back of his hand and took him to Rolex, the famous restaurant on the footpath of the

Odiansalai stadium that was home to late-night clients. It was the only place in Pondicherry where you could find alcohol after 11 p.m. The man sat on the table and ate to his heart's content. When Murugan told him that his bus was going to leave, the villager, who was drunk by now, shooed him away with his hand. He could hardly stand up and was stuttering. He held on steadily to his bag with one hand and tried to adjust his falling *veshti* with the other. He asked Murugan to find him a hotel room and some weed before that.

Viji was woken up in the middle of the night. With heavy-lidded eyes, she got into Murugan's auto-rickshaw. That was their first meeting.

Murugan started his auto-rickshaw. Sitting under the banyan tree, Viji's mother gave him a warning.

'Bring her back as soon as she has finished, all right? No walk in the park and eating *sundal*. You think I don't understand your game? If you think I'll marry my girl to you, you must be dreaming! My Viji is a queen! Do you think I'll get her married to an auto-rickshaw driver?'

Murugan murmured something to himself and gave her his best false smile. Viji sat on the backseat and for the last time looked back at the hut. Her brothers and sisters were innocently playing hopscotch. Watching her leave, they waved. They were jealous of Viji and often complained to their mother: 'Why is only Viji allowed to dress like a queen and do make-up? Why is it always her who goes out with Murugan *Annan*? Why don't we get nice clothes like her?' If only they knew! The young girl looked at them sadly and faded into the distance. She was feeling guilty about leaving them. What will happen to them? Her sisters were so young and innocent; would they have to go through the same fate as her? Was it fair to leave them behind? How would they live without money? The income that Viji brought home was not negligible. Two thousand or three thousand rupees every day was a huge sum in this neighbourhood where the average monthly salary did not go beyond five thousand rupees! Doubt had set in, and she could not continue with this vilifying existence. She felt dirty. When she came back in the evening, she spent hours under the shower, scrubbing herself clean of the dirty human misery she was in. No soap or shampoo could get rid of the dirt in her heart. To reassure herself, she promised to pull them out of this horrible existence as soon as she could.

She did not know whether to laugh or cry when Murugan proposed to her and suggested that she leave her family and live with him. She saw his face in the rear-view mirror of the auto-rickshaw; the melancholic look in his eyes showed sincerity. Not knowing how to answer, Viji sought refuge in an evasive silence. On the way back, Murugan took a detour by the old Governor's Park. Sitting on the lawn, behind the slide-facing Quality Bar, he proposed to her again. Viji stayed silent. She was a little disturbed sitting so close to Murugan. However, she knew men well. Since her teenage years, she was tolerating their dirty bodies, alcoholic breath, their violent and gauche advances. She had seen their embarrassed smiles as they put on their clothes again. But this closeness was somewhat troubling. When she felt Murugan's fingers lightly touch her forearm, she shivered. When he took her hands in his to prove his sincerity, she was overwhelmed and taken aback. Nobody had ever touched her so gently before. Teardrops formed in her eyes, and with the batting of her eyelids, flew out in an emotion that flooded her face and could have dropped on the grass like dew in the night.

Her mother's usual place under the banyan tree was empty. 'Give me some time,' she whispered, clinging onto a tree branch as her toe drew an arc on the ground. Her mother's snoring rose up along with the distant barking of dogs. A little dreamy, she watched him disappear into the night.

Murugan was a fine person: he was loveable and well-mannered. The young girl was not used to such gallantry. Used to insults and altercations in the human jungle that she lived in, the smallest of kind words rang in her ears like a poem. Like Murugan, Viji was not very talkative. They rarely spoke to each other. Their language was silence. She liked his discreet presence. They did not need to talk or express their thoughts. In any case, Murugan spent his time listening to sad old songs by Kannadasan on his rattled radio. Before, she used to ask him to play songs from new and happier movies.

He did not have them. One day, he took her to Burma Bazaar and asked her to choose what she liked. The cassette stayed in his glovebox, still unwrapped. Viji ended up getting used to the depressing music. She even started feeling a little relaxed listening to the sad songs. 'There are people who are sadder than me,' she thought.

The elegiac voice of Chandra Babu ended in the last verse of a sad song by Kannadasan when the auto-rickshaw stopped in front of an isolated little house on the side of the hillock. Viji looked around quickly. A little further away, she saw bright lights and heard the sound of televisions coming from the row of yellow buildings. It was reassuring. Lost in her thoughts, she did not notice the way and did not know which part of the town they were in.

'Come in, Viji. Do not be afraid. From now onwards, this is your home! This is Lawspet, a quiet neighbourhood. Do you see those buildings? They are houses for government officers. All good people!' said Murugan, as he pushed the door open. 'No need to cook tonight, Viji. I will buy some food and be back soon.' Before leaving, he had taken off his uniform and hung it on a nail on the wall to the right. Viji took the jacket and sniffed it. 'It needs to be washed,' she murmured, heading towards the bathroom after closing the door. She smiled graciously.

Knock! Knock! Someone was at the door. Surprised, Viji walked to the entrance. She wiped her soapy hands with the back of her *dhavani* and lifted the door handle.

A man was standing at the threshold.

'Good evening, what do you want?' she asked, somewhat confused to see this visitor so late.

'It is you who I want. Murugan didn't tell you?' asked the man as he entered the room.

'Tell me about what?' enquired Viji with a trembling voice. She stared at him. The man had a satisfied smile on his face. She recognized this type of smile; it was anchored in her memory. This diabolic, leery smile. She had seen it hundreds of times in the darkness of hidden and drab rooms. He was there, in front of her wearing a smile that she wished she would never have to see again. The sadistic predator who entered the room while closing the door behind him wore the hideous mask of a destiny ridden with traps that she thought she had gotten rid of.

'I am the client!' The man's voice rang out like a whip.

Viji's heart stopped beating.

Mani Enna?

Even the ocean did not want to have anything to do with him. The deafening and trembling waves tore through him on the deserted beach. Naked and dislodged, he was getting crushed against the still black rocks that helplessly watched over this macabre scene. His body followed the contours of the waves, drawing on the damp sand enigmatic and ephemerous lines that disappeared even while they were drawn. The cowardly and deadly moonlight withdrew as the first ray of sunlight appeared. It was left up to the accomplice stars to wipe out the last traces of light on this creature who was damned by the gods. Rejecting its crapulous blanket, Pondicherry woke up and got ready to hide behind its faux holy veil.

'*Mani enna*?' Inspector Kadirvel's aggressive tone made his companion jump as he tried to chase the onlookers with his lathi. The inspector had woken up with a start and was in a bad mood. He could have escaped the trial of writing the damned report had the relay arrived on time. As usual, his colleague was late. He scrutinized the long avenue, looking in the direction of the Statue of Dupleix in the hope of spotting Inspector Raj's jeep.

Nothing! Diabetic silhouettes, their sweaty bellies bulging out, were taking long strides along the Cours Chabrol, dreaming of ladoos and jalebis. With a pang of remorse, Kadirvel settled down to write the report, over which he was quite worked up. He didn't really like all this paperwork. The policeman grabbed the pen with which he had just cleaned his ears, wiping it on the sleeve of his crumpled uniform. He looked at his watch to make sure his good-for-nothing assistant, Muthu – whom he hardly trusted – had given him the exact information. He could have checked the time himself when he had reached, but what good was this flunky who spent most of his time shoving his stick in all the orifices of his body?

After a long sigh, he got ready to write his report. But he stopped almost instantly. The aroma of hot masala dosas wafting out from the café set his stomach grumbling with hunger. Strange because he had gobbled down a heap of idlis in the morning from the street vendor at the mobile restaurant in front of the railway station, much to the disgust of the owner, who despised him. The inspector was ruffled and this made him angry, because at times like these he just could not stop eating. He was tempted to send his colleague to get some dosas. He changed his mind when he saw the swelling crowd. He fulminated silently against the bloody waves that had hurled a human body to the shore but had also quietly robbed it of its damaged *kaili*. He would have preferred the opposite to be true.

Refusing to drive or get down from his jeep, he watched the two fishermen struggling to remove the body that was stuck between the rocks. He wanted to finish off with this matter. He had a long day ahead of him. The bus for Salem was leaving in an hour; he would not have the time to go home and change. He reached out for the plastic bag that he was carrying as a precaution, which contained a rolled up messy bundle of civilian clothes. His wife would have a heart attack if she saw this, but since she had left her marital home, Inspector Kadirvel's life had become purgatory. Swallowing his pride, he had decided to bring her back, promising to give her a better life. Caught up in thinking about his wife and distracted by the smell of fresh dosas, he did not notice Inspector Raj's jeep screech to a halt. A wave ran through the crowd as the two fishermen placed the body at the base of the statue. Curious onlookers crowded behind the police cordon on tiptoe, trying to get a better look.

Kadirvel was talking to his colleague when his assistant discreetly beckoned him to come behind one of the pillars of the statue.

Panic struck across Muthu's bony face.

'Sir, the body…'

'What about the body?' asked the inspector, a little irritated.

'The body, it's... the young man you manhandled last evening.'

'*Mani enna*?'

Old Anjamma was standing at the entrance, asking Jaffar the tailor the same question for the nth time. He had finished opening his little shop situated on the *thinnai* of his neighbour's house and was busy praying with closed eyes in front of an image of the Karaikal *dargah*. He did not like being interrupted. Irritated, he opened his eyes after a few minutes of silence and glanced at the dusty old clock ticking away on a cracked wall but did not answer. Anjamma sighed with sadness. She went up to the sidewalk and looked beyond the street, hoping to see Jacques. Rue de Bussy woke up brutally. Anjamma saw a crowded JVS bus go by, carrying a load of passengers hanging from its doors. The horn of the newspaper delivery man burst out furiously every time he stopped by clients. Fishmongers, arguing loudly, were headed towards the Petit Bazaar. Their language was so obscene that even their fish rotted away petrified while listening to it. Schoolchildren from the Jayarani High School, in blue and white uniforms, rushed by taking short, quick steps. The last bell announcing the beginning of classes rang in the old woman's ears.

Worried as she was, Anjamma decided to return. She hesitated and was tempted to ask Jaffar one last time what time it was. But she changed her mind looking at the gruff face of the old Muslim who seemed to be ignoring her. She stopped in front of Jacques's open room and looking at his unslept mat, a strange feeling swept over her. She was used to hearing his soft steps when he returned tired and exhausted, bringing in the fragrance of his forbidden love. A dark emotion arose inside her as she headed towards the backyard to heat some water. Jacques was used to taking a bath as soon as he got up. She took some dry *filao*s and placed them under the copper pot. The wood caught fire instantly. The fine bark crackled and gave out small sparks which escaped, taking with them the troubled thoughts of the old woman.

Anjamma was happy when the young man arrived at her home that night of Bhogi. Apart from the tiny pile of threadbare linen she had collected over the year, she had nothing else to burn. Only the bitter smoke of the brazier could have given her the pleasure of crying. Life had filled her with so much bitterness, her sadness had dried up her eyes. Her long solitary life had only been a dry desert where feelings evaporated in an emotional mirage. Her husband, a useless alcoholic, had abandoned her very early to be among drunks and pimps in the lowest of dungeons in Pondicherry. Abandoned by her family, poor Anjamma had to struggle from a very young age to bring up her only daughter in a dignified manner. From being a maid, an employee at the railways to being a cleaner at the toilets in front of the distillery, her entire life was thrown into a dark pit of humanity, just to make sure her daughter had a better future. In this society, where ugliness was hereditary, her battle against destiny was titanic. But she had won!

Her daughter was well-educated and had found a well-paid job in Madras. She left her mother, promising to pull her out of her miserable condition as soon as possible. But that day did not come so soon. For months and years, Anjamma waited at the threshold of the house. Her poor little bundle, hidden behind the door, a cruel reminder. Abandoned and disabled, poor Anjamma collapsed in deep sadness. One monsoon evening, a shiny Ambassador stopped in front of her house. The old woman, who was busy arranging her aluminium pots on the floor of her bedroom, stopped right away. The damaged tiled roof leaked heavily under the relentless rainfall, flooding the dark little room. The sound of rain falling on the utensils created an unbearable deafening ruckus. When the driver entered the room, Anjamma was completely drenched and shivering in the cold.

Ayah! That is what they called her in the new household where she was brought in through the backdoor on that rainy night. *Ayah* is the maid who does everything. Anjamma had been the cook, guard, servant and nanny. This was why her daughter made her come to Madras: to take care of her new-born baby that she couldn't raise alone. Busy with evening parties at the Rotary Club with her rich husband, coupled with her insatiable desire to travel, Anjamma's daughter did not want to play the role of a mother. Raising the child was beyond her. The ungrateful daughter who had forgotten her own mother, remembered her well when in need. For as long as she lived with her daughter and looked after her grandson, old Anjamma eagerly accepted her new life instead of thinking about her past, doing miserable menial tasks living in the back garden of the Adyar villa.

A few years later, a Maruti dropped her off like a pile of dirty linen in front of the house. Anjamma's heart was heavy. She had cried endlessly for days thinking about the separation that was drawing closer. In spite of her humiliating condition, the old woman was passionately attached to her grandson, Arjuna. She would have preferred dying as a servant in her daughter's house instead of coming back to live in Pondicherry. But destiny would have it otherwise.

'*Mani enna*?' Jacques asked the question for the third time to the young man sitting on the ledge, a little further from Gandhi's statue. He looked lost in his thoughts, staring at the sea. In a temper, he turned to Jacques.

'If you ask me this question again, I'll break your head against the wall, like a coconut. What do you want, you bloody…'

He did not finish his sentence. Terrified, Jacques distanced himself quickly. With his left hand, he gripped his *kaili* and folded it above his knees to walk faster. A sudden gust of wind swept over the Cours Chabrol. Dark clouds appeared, hurriedly eclipsing the moon and slowly drowning the seafront in darkness. The damaged street lamps lit up here and there erratically, desperately blinking before dying out. Jacques did not know where to go. He walked instinctively towards the distillery. He immediately regretted going in that direction. But it was too late.

Like a zombie, and in spite of himself, he headed towards the cursed street. He had promised himself never to go back there. He stopped for a moment in front of the Selvaraj Mansion to take shelter from the rain. Onlookers hurrying towards the verandah looked at him suspiciously. A little discouraged, he made his way out again. This time, he had his *kaili* wrapped around his legs because of the blowing wind and merciless rain which was now coming down heavily. This gave him a peculiar gait.

Leaning on the wall of the Institut Français, Jacques closed his eyes thinking about his cancelled plan. His heart was heavy, and he felt betrayed. Tears rolled down his face and mingled with the rain. A dog sleeping on the footpath looked at him sadly. Rue Dupuy was plunged into darkness. The dirty stench of urine and faeces did not help. He was used to it. The absence of residential buildings after Rue Saint Louis and Cours Chabrol led to this side of the neighbourhood being abandoned and occupied by the waifs and strays of the Boulevard Nord. Thugs, pimps and dealers of forbidden pleasures had made their home in this stinking street. The face of vice and abjection reigned in this infamous place. Naturally, Jacques had found a haven where he could quench his sexual thirst. Every wall he leaned against transformed itself into a vertical nuptial bed, as a dodgy homage to his temporary lovers.

Jacques. That was not even his name. His parents called him Arjuna. But everybody called him Jacques, referring to his homosexuality. So, Arjuna became Jacques to live up to his nickname. His simple and happy life plunged into hell the day his sexuality became known. Fearing dishonour, his mother hurriedly sent him to Anjamma to carry the burden of shame on her poor old shoulders. Disoriented and disturbed, the young man was happy to find his old ayah. He felt relieved when he met Manivannan. Finally, his turbulent life got a moment of respite.

The last two cancelled dates had not ruffled him. He knew that Manivannan often disappeared to his *therukoothu* shows. This was how they had met. He was attracted by his beauty and talent when the troupe came to perform at the Draupadi temple of Murungapakkam. Since then, Manivannan came to see him whenever he could take a few days off. On his last visit, Manivannan promised him a happy life together.

Their third meeting was a disaster and that had troubled him. Feeling betrayed, Jacques stood still, not knowing what to do. The rain redoubled with force, pouring tears on this unsure miserable being shivering in the cold. Even the old drenched dog left his spot seeking shelter.

A vehicle screeched to a halt, shaking him out of his state. It reversed and stopped in front of him. Jacques recognized the police jeep. He was scared. He clung onto his *kaili* with his left hand and with his right hand blocked his face from the glaring headlights.

'What are you doing there, you dirty little faggot?' The inspector's voice cut through the sound of the rain.

'Nothing, Inspector, I am waiting for a friend.' His shy voice was lost in the clap of thunder.

'What?' shouted the inspector. 'I can't hear anything. Come closer!'

Petrified, Jacques could hardly blink. In spite of the inspector's orders, he couldn't move. A heavy silence fell upon the street. A few seconds later the door of the jeep banged noisily. Jacques shivered as the man slapped him. He tried to protect himself, but in vain. The man slapped him twice and holding his arms behind his back brought him in front of the inspector.

'*Pottai thevudiya*! What are you doing so late on the streets? Even in this bad weather, you are roaming around to get laid! Come, little faggot, I'll satisfy you!'

The policeman pushed him against the wall and pulled his *kaili* down. Jacques started crying and fell on his knees, begging to be let go. A diabolic look gleamed on the inspector's face as lightning struck in the dark sky. He unbuttoned his pants and grabbed Jacques's head. He forced the boy to bend. As the young boy resisted, he kicked him in the chest and threw him against the wall. The boy was on all fours trying hard to get up. Another kick in the ribs forced him to lie down like a dog. He fainted as he felt the *lathi* enter his body.

'*Mani enna*?'

A cowardly moon, completely disgusted by so much abjection, hid behind the clouds.

'*Mani enna*?'

Like vulgar lights on a morbid scene, the stars stopped shining one by one, plunging into a universe of obscure anguish.

'*Mani enna*?'

Standing on the rock, facing the ocean, Jacques uttered his pick-up line one last time. Like a broken and ephemeral pendulum, he swung his body into the emptiness.

The Exile

Lourdenadin was sadly contemplating the end of the rainfall. In the glow of the lamp, he watched the raindrops dwindle and become thinner and lighter. Rue Montorsier was slowly coming back to life. The first clients of Amnivasam arrived stealthily. After parking their motorcycles at the corner of the Ellaiamman Koil Street, they trooped quickly into the bar, not wanting to get wet. People who had taken shelter in the verandahs of neighbouring houses walked towards the street, their hands extended outwards to feel the falling rain which could stop their drenched bikes, while others found their way again, pants and *veshti*s rolled up their legs. They were taking long strides to avoid the puddles, their left arms behind their backs to protect their watches from the rain. Wet dogs barked as they watched cows carelessly roaming around in the flooded streets, looking for food amid the waste.

Lourdenadin paced up and down the footpath of Senthil Real Estate, smoking his last cigarette to control his impatience. He looked at the hideous clock of the real estate agency which now showed 8 p.m. It had been more than an hour since he had been waiting for the manager. Through the cigarette smoke, he saw a young girl stop in front of the blue house across the street. She took off her raincoat and waited for the door to open. A smiling woman came out to let her in. She helped her carry the canvas bag the girl was holding. The woman stopped for a moment with a friendly nod, to which he replied politely. A delicious aroma wafted out of the half-open kitchen. 'My god! What a divine combination!' he thought. *Meen kuzhambu*, *sura puttu* and steamed rice. He looked longingly at the door behind the two women and went into the tiny office of the agency.

The employee and his nephew stared at the television screen in complete adulation at a certain Vijay, who was making grotesque moves in a snowy Swiss landscape. The dumbfounded Tyroleans ogled at the heroine, who was clad in a carelessly flowing sari. Without taking his eyes off the screen, the boy pushed a chair towards Lourdenadin.

'Sit down, sir. *Annan* will be here soon.'

Lourdenadin could hardly hear him and sat down patiently. He had been listening to the same song on the television for an hour. He looked at the small igloo-like room. In spite of the rain, the air conditioner was on full blast and the young man refused to turn it off. '*Annan* will scold me if I switch it off,' he explained. Lourdenadin shivered a bit and tucked his legs under his thighs to warm them up. He sighed in exasperation and looked around the office. On the right wall was a framed collage of photos. The pot-bellied manager could be seen posing with politicians, actors and celebrities. In one picture, he was giving a hug to a minister with a pretentious smile. In another one, he was garlanding an actor who looked as moronic as him. Further on, he was standing in front of the Eiffel Tower, the London Bridge and other monuments from the world over. He seemed to look important in all his Kollywoodian poses.

After careful scrutiny, Lourdenadin realised that these were computerized photos. The wall on the left was covered with portraits of Hindu deities adorned with fresh garlands. Apart from a telephone covered in plastic, the table was empty. A dirty-looking towel was spread on his faux-leather office chair. Everything in this agency was repulsive: the kitsch decor, the noisy television, the heavy smell of incense and the cold. More than anything, he was appalled by the *Maneki-neko* and the fat laughing Buddha on the shelf behind the chair. The golden cat with its repetitive movements made him feel like grabbing its paw. He got up, stretched and walked out.

He took out a packet of cigarettes and realized that it was empty. He crumpled it with his right hand and threw it away, feeling tired. He looked around. A shop was open on Mahatma Gandhi Road. He gravitated towards it. Something struck him, and he walked back instead. He picked up the packet of cigarettes he had thrown. He looked at an old man who was smoking a *suruttu* peacefully on the *thinnai* of Villa Mano. He pointed towards a round cement trash can almost accusingly. Lourdenadin threw the packet there and instinctively walked towards the bar. While waiting for his order, his thoughts went back to the past.

'This was all I could get, son.' His father put a small canvas bag from Silk Palace down. It was full of dirty torn banknotes. The young man sitting on the small *thinnai* of the mud house jumped up! He had been dreaming of his father returning all day.

His mind was racing, thinking about a country he knew only by name: France! A country, a mirage, an El Dorado they had been tempting him with since childhood. It was easy to get to the oh-so-desirable France. The French government would pay for his ticket, but a small amount of money was still required. He needed shoes, a suitcase, a suit, warm clothes, and, of course, some cash. The joy of getting the news about his military service was only short-lived. The exhaustive list of things he needed to buy was drawn up by an old soldier in the village, and it had plunged his father in deep worry. Where would he find the money to buy all this?

After a few trips to town, he had come back home empty-handed, where Lourdenadin was waiting impatiently. Unable to find a solution, the old man had been forced to sell his small rice field. That was the money he had given to his son.

Gandhi's toothless smile on the dirty banknotes could not hide the sadness welling up inside the two men.

The tinkling of the Amrut glass on the table shook him out of his torpor. The waiter offered him a packet of Gold Flake and he stood up, scratching his head. Lourdenadin paid the bill and asked the waiter to keep the change. Happy with the tip, he came back with a little bowl of roasted peanuts. Lourdenadin wanted to place another order but changed his mind. He had found a table far from the crowd and especially away from the television. His thoughts went out of the window, mingling with the chain of memories that the waiter had interrupted.

He had had tears in his eyes when he left his small village, Murungapakkam. The green rice fields were only a faded image now. The sound of the bell in the small Saint Xavier chapel was only a distant echo now; the breeze from the coconut tree could not put him to sleep anymore. Even the sound of children playing and chasing the cowherd returning from the fields at sunset would no longer resonate in his ears. The silhouettes of ravishing women leaving the fountain in the fields would leave his memory soon. Eventually, the moringa would become phantoms that were to haunt him in the cold nights in that faraway land.

The day he had left, the entire village seemed to have descended on his humble home. The elders sat on a bed of coconut leaves on the *thinnai*, talking about everything and nothing, calling him time and again to give him advice. The women gave him blessings, sitting on the same floor as the group of mourners. When the taxi arrived, the children shouted and ran towards the vehicle, throwing out a cloud of smoke and dust. It was not an ordinary taxi; due to the dearth of money his father had arranged for the old Dodge from the Dhandabani company that was used to transport sound and light equipment. As soon as the vehicle parked at the entrance of the village, young and old people ran towards it, clambering for a place to sit. What a racket they had made!

He had realized that he was leaving the country the moment they had reached Maduranthakam. It was the last stop for all travellers leaving for Madras. In this tiny street full of watering holes and tea shops, his father took him aside under the big tamarind tree. He took his hands, his eyes full of tears, his voice trembling.

'I am sad to see you go, son. But do we have a choice? I would have really wanted you to study and become successful. But destiny wanted otherwise. I know you are worried, Lourdes. You are the first one in the family to go so far; the only one who is going to a faraway country where we do not know anyone. I feel guilty about putting this weight on your young shoulders. But I am not worried about you. You were always a docile, gentle and respectful boy. You take your responsibilities seriously. If you do not succeed for one reason or another, it is not a problem. I only want you to be happy. God is with us!' With a trembling hand, he reached under his *veshti* and pulled out something from the pocket of his striped shorts. It was a brand new faux leather pouch.

'Here you are, my son! This is all I have and this is all we are left with. Centuries of work is in your hands. Put it to good use. Go and see your mother now and reassure her.'

For the first time in his life, Lourdenadin looked straight into his father's eyes and said, 'I promise you, Father, I will do my best, and I will succeed. Don't worry, from now onwards I will look after the family. The ancestral land that you have sacrificed for me and the family will not go in vain. As soon as I start earning enough money, we will buy it back and you will be proud of me. I promise you in the name of our ancestors!'

His old father took him by his shoulders. His sad eyes looked at him with tenderness and pride. He dusted his son's new suit and without saying anything went behind the tamarind tree to cry, tears rolling down his cheeks. As Lourdenadin got closer to Meenambakkam Airport, he felt strangely relieved when he went past the entry gate. The image of his father holding his mother by the shoulders with his three sisters and his little brother stayed etched in his memory.

Lourdenadin would have never imagined that one day he would go so far – to a country called France. In spite of the many promises his father made since he was a child, a life outside Pondicherry was unimaginable. It was with a heavy heart that he let himself be admitted to the French school. But the old peasant had a plan in his head. He did not want his children to go through the same experiences as he did. It was time to escape the clutches of destiny. The old man was one out of five thousand people who had opted for French citizenship in 1962. He was among those who dreamt of changing their destiny with a thumbprint on a piece of paper. He was devoted, indebted and the target of ridicule in the village for enrolling his son Lourdenadin in a French school. He had put all he had in this much-wanted child and named him Lourdenadin to thank Our Lady of Lourdes in Villianur, who had answered his prayers by giving him a son after two daughters. The saint had shown her grace. Had she not come to help Dr Lephine's daughter in Thambusamy Mudaliar and to the thousands of pilgrims who came to worship her? In 1867, the Society of Foreign Missions of Paris decided to build a chapel and bought some land in Kanuvapet. Ten years later, the church was built under the supervision of Reverend Tharbes, who was a distant cousin of Bernadette Soubirous. People deemed it a miracle when the statue reached the cathedral intact, after having fallen three times. Who would have imagined that it was thanks to the skills of Lourdenadin's great grandfather, the transporter, that the statue was saved on 7 April 1877? The Virgin was indebted to him!

An uncommon willpower pushed the old man to follow his dreams. Their wealth in Kothadimai had dried up with his father who succeeded in buying a plot of land that was tilled by the family. Lourdenadin's father worked hard to get rid of the injustices of the world, stuck to them for centuries. Money was the only means. Prosperity was to be found only in France. He knew that the society in which he was born was controlled by the caste system, and he could not live a good life in his village.

In spite of his wife's reluctance, he did not hesitate to take a loan, so that Lourdenadin could get a good education. He had run for 6 kilometres to look at his son's CEP results. The huge building of the Calve College, built in 1875 at the site of an old cemetery, amazed him. He went and sat down next to the Chettiar tea shop to light a beedi. He did not dare show up at the main entrance of the school where all his son's friends would be, ashamed that his clothes were smelling of mud and straw.

Leaning on the wall of the Mailam monastery, he prayed to Saint Francis Xavier to come to his rescue. He cried tears of joy when Lourdenadin showed him his name in the list of students who had passed. He had known tears of sadness and despair, but these were tears of happiness rolling down his dirty cheeks. They tasted like exquisite nectar. Lourdenadin had kept his promise. He had come back five years later and purchased the land that his father had sold. He remembered the pride on his father's face when he brought the buyer to his newly built house to give him the laminated documents. The following day, the old man had taken him by the arm to their land next to the *filao*s rattan plantation. He grabbed a handful of earth, said a short prayer with closed eyes and then drew a cross on his forehead. With frail and tired arms, he hugged his son, kissing him with affection. Lourdenadin was surprised and troubled by all this love. He had only known the strict and authoritarian ways of his father until now.

The young man was tired but happy in front of the crowd of villagers gathered there for their gifts. They left smiling after blessing him, carrying back sweets, Saint Michel soaps, eau de cologne. All day long, you could hear the music playing in the courtyard on the new music system, but the sound of children shouting with joy completely drowned it. His mother gave gifts to the people tirelessly working in the kitchen. The aroma of *varutha kari*, *kari vathal*, chicken *kurma*, biryani and other tasty dishes floated everywhere. Dass, the village cook, was employed full-time in the house. In the lacklustre hut where once they quickly lapped up *kanji* in aluminium plates, now glasses tinkled with cutlery. His father showed off his new ring with tricoloured precious stones that his son had gifted him. He now spent his days on the big *thinnai* with his friends, drinking whisky and smoking Caporal. At nightfall, the old peasant and his son sat on the terrace under the open sky, gazing over the vast rice fields that they planned to buy.

Lourdenadin's life was all about sacrifice. But for him, it was a duty. In a few years, he had bought some land, married his three sisters into good families, paid for his brother's studies so he could become a professor at a high school in Bordeaux and make his parents proud. His hard work and perseverance had made him an officer who was liked and respected by his colleagues. Lourdenadin had just taken retirement after twenty-seven years of a military career and had only dreamt of one thing: leaving! Going back home to his birthplace where the fresh breeze of the rice fields had seen him come into this world. His feet, trapped in Rangers for decades now, wanted to unfurl on the hot earth he had worked on with his father. He wanted to build a beautiful house along the Ariyankuppam River, to savour nightfall in the light breeze and listen to the gentle croaking of frogs. Unfortunately, his wife refused to leave the beautiful house in Montlhéry under the pretext of educating their children. She countered Lourdenadin's arguments and plans of returning home. In reality, she also wanted to come back to Pondicherry, but the prospect of her children spending the rest of their lives sharing Lourdenadin's pension with the rest of the family scared her.

Since they had become somewhat prosperous, relatives had mushroomed out of nowhere. Cousins, aunts and uncles that Lourdenadin had never known came to their home over vacations, asking for gifts and money. What made them happy exasperated his wife and children, who thought their return to paradise would soon become a living hell. Once again, Lourdenadin made a sacrifice. He had always lived in the hope of returning home one day but instead he found a job at the town hall in Montlhéry. His children had grown up, were married and had started their own families. The second retirement was upon him.

Lourdenadin signalled to the waiter for another drink and looked at his watch. He had been sitting in the bar for half an hour and there was no news from the real estate agent. It kept him calm because he could think of other things. He looked at his watch again, his gaze fixed on the dial. Thirty minutes – his life relived in only thirty minutes. Fifty years of hard work, devotion and sacrifice reduced to thirty minutes! Every hour, minute and second and fragment of time had been sacrificed for the family. What had he done with his life? Even if the satisfaction of fulfilling his duties took over him, he sometimes felt despair. He would resign himself to that condition if he had had a moment of respite in this life lived for others. But his dreams were shattered to pieces when he got together with his family to celebrate his retirement.

'But what do you want to do there alone, Papa?' his son asked him irritably. 'You have been singing the same song for half a century! Leave, leave, leave! What will you do there? Your family is here!'

'Yes, but that is where I come from, Yvon. My country is India, my son,' answered Lourdenadin, his eyes sad.

'India, what do you know about India, Papa? Apart from Pondicherry and Velankanni, you know nothing about India. India is not your country. You have lived in France longer than in India. Your country is France!'

'I was born there. My native land is Pondicherry. That is the land of your ancestors, don't ever forget that!' He felt an anger rising in him. He looked at his children, one by one, in the hope of getting some support. His daughter came close to him and gently tried taking the glass of whisky he was holding in his hand; she was scared that the conversation might turn into a fight. He looked at her, exasperated and gripped the glass with all his might.

'Land of your ancestors! Papa, Murungapakkam is a little village. There is nothing there anymore! When you were young, there were rice fields and farm land, but today it is barren land on which they have built ugly houses. Is that your village?'

'What do you know about my village? Murungapakkam has existed since the time of the Tamil Sangam and heroes in the *Purananuru*...'

'Papa, I am not here to listen to history lessons nor the tale of the past glory of your village,' Yvon replied dryly.

The younger one was playing with his newborn and handed him over to his wife, making his way to the table to sit next to his brother.

'Yvon is right, Papa. You have nothing to do there all alone. Who will look after you?'

'But I am not going to go there alone. Your mother will be there!' he replied, irritated.

'Be reasonable, Papa! This is not the first time we are talking about this,' said the elder one. 'My mother does not want to go far from us. Isn't that true, Ma?'

Busy cooking, their mother pretended not to listen. Torn between her love for her children and her husband's love for his native village and all the sacrifices he had made, she preferred to stay quiet. She knew how strongly her husband felt about this, but the thought of living so far from her children saddened her.

'You cannot understand.' Looking towards the kitchen for a brief moment, Lourdenadin hoped for the support of his wife. 'I was snatched from my land at an early age to come here and make a living. I lived my whole life in exile, far from my near and dear ones, far from my village. Even after all these years, I have a strange feeling of not belonging to this country. You will never understand.' His voice was breaking with sadness and anger. 'I might be French, but my soul is Indian! I want to die there. I want to breathe my last in the breeze of my lost rice fields.'

'That's it! You are becoming emotional now,' retorted Yvon, looking up at the ceiling.

'Yes, emotional. If I wasn't emotional, you wouldn't be here! It is because I had these feelings that I could bring up this family so well. I made sacrifices to give all of you a good life and an honourable death to my parents. I never complained because this was my duty. It is because of this sense of duty that I want to return to my country. Have you ever been deprived of anything? I could have gone and settled in Pondicherry after retiring from the army, but I didn't. Why? Because I cared about you. To make sure you had a happy childhood and a good education, so that you could become someone in society. Don't I have the right to now live a peaceful life and die where I belong?'

A disturbing silence fell over the living room. Yvon turned to the television. It was getting on his nerves. He grabbed the remote and switched it off.

'Why are you switching the TV off? Can't you see that I am watching it?' scolded Lourdenadin.

'But we are talking, Papa! Anyway, who watches Michel Drucker?!' joked the young man, trying to ease the situation.

'I do! I am in my home and can do what pleases me. I don't need ungrateful children to tell me what I should do,' he added.

'Ungrateful! Us? Your brothers and sisters are ungrateful! We only think about your wellbeing. We want to look after you and Ma. We want you to live close to your grandchildren. We want you to teach them the same values and give them the same love that you gave us. Is that being ungrateful?'

'What do my brothers and sisters have to do with this?' he asked, tired. He was not on good terms with them and that made him sad.

'We are not the ones asking you for our share of inheritance. You are the one who bought all these houses and land with your own money. You sacrificed to give them a better life. You married your sisters off to respectable families; you brought them to France and helped them settle down here. What did you get in return? Nothing. Your brother, a professor, lived with you until he became independent. You paid for his studies and brought him up like your son, and now? Mr Professor thinks you are a lowly peasant and doesn't even meet you. They are ungrateful! Not us, Papa! And most of all, they have the gall to ask for their inheritance!'

Yvon banged his glass down on the table and left the room.

The short moment of silence was interrupted by public

applause. Michel Drucker welcomed Mimie Mathy for the umpteenth time. Lourdenadin leaned his head back on the sofa and closed his eyes. Jean Pierre came closer and put his hand on his father's knee reassuringly.

'It's better if you resolve this issue soon, Papa. Go back home, sell the land and the houses and come back for an easy retirement close to us. We want you to be happy. Anyway, what is becoming of all the land that you bought? Nothing. It is abandoned. Nobody is tilling it. Your family is using you by usurping money for some expense or the other. If you don't sell those houses, they will be occupied by village hoodlums, like hundreds of Franco-Pondicherrian properties. Be practical, Papa.'

When his nephew came, Lourdenadin was undone. Drinking had not helped. On the contrary, he was even more doubtful and troubled. The night before, while looking through all his property papers, he realized that everything was in his name. The old peasant was rewarded and had understood life.

Indecisively, he followed the young boy and entered the real estate agency. The pot-bellied manager was watching the news on the local channel, which was showing floods caused by heavy rains. Without switching the television off, he apologised profusely, blaming the storm for being late. He clumsily took the documents and sifted through them, the big rings on his fingers shining. Lourdenadin let him look through the documents and watched the screen. An angry old farmer was speaking heatedly to a journalist.

'Where would we be without these farming lands that has fed us for centuries? In the name of development, everyone is selling rice fields and agricultural land for money. What will you eat tomorrow? Banknotes? What will our future be if everyone started living in concrete jungles? Will we become labourers on the streets? What will happen to the green spaces? How will you breathe? In olden days, Ozhukarai, Murungapakkam, Kombakkam and all the neighbouring villages were the breadbasket of this city. What did you do to them? Unplanned residential colonies! Ponds, lakes, streams were dried up to build nagars. The inhabitants, like the bureaucrats and politicians, were all corrupt and preferred to sell agricultural land for cash sitting in bank lockers. At the slightest rainfall, your cities get flooded. What is the government doing? They reimburse you to keep quiet until the next rainfall and continue with even bigger illegal constructions. You are just a headless herd!'

'Switch off the TV, stupid idiot!' yelled the agency owner, turning to his employee.

Lourdenadin smiled mysteriously. He stared long at the dark screen where the silhouette of the farmer disappeared. He seemed to think a bit and then got up from his chair. Without saying a word, he started collecting his scattered documents before putting them back in his brown bag.

'What are you doing, sir? Are you leaving?' asked the manager, a bit troubled.

'Yes, I am leaving. My property is not for sale anymore,' said Lourdenadin calmly.

'But... You're making a big mistake. Land in Murungapakkam is much sought after. I can sell it for you at a good price. Trust me. I am the best. Moreover, an art and craft village is coming up close to your land. It will go up in value. Think again, sir!'

The manager was almost begging. He looked surprised and angry at Lourdenadin's nephew who had brought him there. His nephew had been calm until now, but now, on seeing his commission disappear, he began panicking. He could see his money disappear.

'Uncle, wait! What is the problem? We haven't even started negotiating. Be patient! I will get you a good price.'

'My land and houses have no price. Come on! Let's go!' Lourdenadin headed towards the door.

The young man was stuck, glued to his chair. Lourdenadin walked back, took the keys of the motorbike and went down the stairs. His nephew lost his temper.

'But what are you doing, Uncle? Are you going to ride my mobike? You don't even know how to!'

Lourdenadin went up to the motorbike. He put his bag on the rack close to the tank, cleaned the seat and sat on it. A Bullet! He had dreamt of riding one when he was young! He turned the key on the automatic start. Dha... dha... dha... It came to life with its signature sound. Without waiting for an answer, the Bullet went towards Cours Chabrol, leaving behind the fragrance of a new life.

Malarvizhi

A few drops of blood mingled with the sea water and fell on the wet flowers. Torn from the garland, scattered on the naked rock, the jasmine flowers looked like glistening tears from that deadly night. *I was terrified, horrified by the monstrosity of the act I had just committed. At the same time, I could not stop admiring my courage and savouring my freedom. What a strange sensation it was to do something freeing and independent! In the beginning, I thought I was dreaming. When I touched the rock with both my hands, I was sure it was a dream. I had never imagined that one day I would be capable of doing something like this all by myself!*

Not that it was my ambition; I was pushed by destiny to regain my dignity since that wretched day. It all started on that day of Maasi Magam. *Like every year, the beautifully decorated chariot of Mailam was the first one to be installed on the beach. Pilgrims and vagabonds flocked to place their offerings on it and receive the blessings of Murugan.* Under the strict supervision of his father, Ashwin tried to do his best. It was the first time that he was officiating as the main priest. He couldn't afford to lose his composure in front of thousands of devotees gathered around the chariot. It was especially important to stay alert and be available to satisfy the dignitaries making their way through the crowd arrogantly and piously. *I was also extremely busy following all the directions attentively. Swayed by the crowd, I tried to do my job for better or for worse under the circumstances. All this was tiring me out, for, unlike Ashwin who loved this ambience, I preferred the peace and quiet of the small Muthumariamman Kovil Temple where my family had officiated for generations. These three days of celebrations were a task that I would have gladly forsaken. I knew something was going to happen when the chariot entered the narrow street in front of the elephant-shaped tree. I had a strange feeling that I had been there before, a déjà vu. As much as I disliked this neighbourhood, I never got tired of admiring the old banyan tree which looked so much like an elephant, a symbol of Lord Ganesha. The little street was so narrow that we almost brushed against the pilgrims standing on the threshold of houses to watch the idols pass by. The procession moved forward like a tortoise under the stifling heat. Just when I was praying that it would move faster, our chariot stopped abruptly at the street of flower vendors. Across the street, a cow lying on the road was blocking the way. The agitated organisers and vagabonds could not do anything. The animal refused to budge.* It was then that

Ashwin's gaze fell upon Malarvizhi. She was standing in front of her hut, holding offerings in a straw basket. She seemed to hesitate, overwhelmed by Murugan's chariot. Next to her, a middle-aged woman pushed forth to perform puja. She knew that the young priest was staring at her, but did not dare look him in the eye. After a few minutes – which felt like an eternity – she pulled herself together and shyly approached the chariot around which pilgrims were flocking. In spite of the milling crowds, Ashwin had eyes only for Malarvizhi. Seduced by her beauty, the young man hurriedly did away with the devotees to get closer to her. Malarvizhi's jasmine garland got stuck in Ashwin's *poonul* as she got down from the chariot, jolted forth by the moving procession.

I trembled in horror the first time Malarvizhi touched me. I can't remember how many times I washed myself to get rid of that shameful feeling sticking not only to my skin, but also to my soul. I was horrified and deeply disgusted by the touch of a pariah. I was mortified when her body brushed against me under the elephant tree. I could see her, feel her behind me.

The moment was etched in my memory. On their first meeting, the two lovers met at the small temple in VOC Nagar. Their passionate gazes crossed and embraced without them having to move. The night fell slowly on the dim neighbourhood. Apart from the lamp at the corner of the street, opposite the elephant tree, the street of flower vendors was plunged in darkness. A few oil lamps on the *thinnai* fluttered gently in the wind. Then the dreaded moment arrived. Pretending to pray, Ashwin and Malarvizhi came out of the temple to perform the ritual around the tree to get closer.

She had surely felt my fear and repulsion towards her in the first few minutes. I knew she was watching my slightest movements and expressions to touch me. Ashwin slowed down to let Malarvizhi come closer. She hesitated for a minute and then shyly, and a bit afraid, came and stood next to him. *I could feel her. Then, she touched my foot with hers. An electric current ran through my body which stiffened. Stuck between her and the two lovers, I let myself be humiliated without defending myself.*

Malarvizhi was soft and reserved, but she was also empowering. All my efforts to avoid her were in vain. I understood from the beginning that she felt a naughty pleasure in touching me at the slightest excuse. She took all the chances to brush against me. In Bharathi Park, in the cafés, on the bicycle, on the beachfront, in movie halls, everywhere… I was a prisoner in her hands. She would not let me go. It became unbearable. Swallowing my hate, I continued to bear this assault in silence, not knowing how to complain. What could I do? I could not live without Ashwin. He and I were tied together by an eternal bond.

I found Ashwin's love for Malarvizhi impossible to understand and unthinkable. The dear son of Nilakanta Shastri, the erudite brahmin admired by his community for his knowledge and observance of dharmic rules, in love with a pariah? Just the thought of it disgusted me. If the priest discovered this, he would die of shame. But the possibility of a family disaster did not bother Ashwin. Blinded by this nonsensical love, he was capable of sacrificing his family's honour. Nothing could stop him. *I could not let him carry on like this.*

'Are you sure, Ashwin?' The question was lost in the noise of the waves crashing against the rocks. Malarvizhi stared at Ashwin's confident face, shining under the full moon. Torn between admiration and doubt, the young girl did not know what to say when Ashwin proposed they elope and get married at the Mailam Temple. After three years of a clandestine relationship, the young boy, not wanting to reveal his love to his parents, decided to get married secretly. Worried about their future, the two lovers planned their elopement in detail, sitting on the rocks of the Keerapalayam jetty. *As usual, I watched them from a distance.*

Naturally, she was there too. Sitting by my side, she watched me, waiting for one thing only: to touch me. The beach was deserted. There was only the sound of the sea that broke the heavy silence. A huge wave came and crashed against the rocks. Frightened, Malarvizhi hid in Ashwin's arms. *She was waiting only for this and came and hid in my arms. I was horrified! Even after three years, I was not used to this dirty touch. Instinctively, I wanted to push her into the sea to get rid of her forever.*

Alas, I wasn't free to do that. Disgusted and stuck, I let myself be polluted without having the courage to defend myself. But at the bottom of my heart, I knew this had to end. I could not let them get married. I could not put up with this humiliation for the rest of my life. Enough was enough! I had to do something! But, what? Doubt clouded my mind and the fear of having to live with her for the rest of my life desperately drove me to put an end to this monstrosity.

There was a full moon, but darkness fell upon the tiny fisherman's village. Night fell quietly to liberate the hidden and forbidden desires of the two lovers. Ashwin locked his gaze with Malarvizhi's and took her in his arms. A black cloud floated by to gently kiss the round face of the moon. Darkness… Malarvizhi shivered with pleasure when Ashwin put his lips on hers. Petrified… *I was going berserk watching this. She kissed me passionately for long as if wanting to suck out my dirtied soul. Horror!* Ashwin ran his hand over Malarvizhi's body.

Disgust… She came to give more of herself to me. Repulsion… She took me by the neck and pulled me towards her. I wanted to get rid of her and escape. But how? It was then that the unimaginable happened. I managed to pull out of her clutches and push her away. She was taken aback. My first instinct was to look at Ashwin and Malarvizhi. They were still intertwined, lost in eternal love. She couldn't understand why Ashwin's shadow had pulled away. She was lost. Without wasting time, I wanted to run away. To go where? Not too far. Ashwin would catch up with me pretty soon. A demonic idea came to me. For as long as Ashwin was alive, I would never be free. I had to do everything I could to stop this marriage. I thought of my father, Nilakanta Shastri, and my family. I could not leave them to live with the shame and disappear after the scandal. The heavy rock shook in my hands.

Some drops of blood mingled with the seawater and fell on the wet flowers. Torn from the garland, scattered on the naked rock, the jasmine flowers now looked like luminescent tears of a deathly night. The two bodies lay stuck between the rocks, battered by the waves. *I was disgusted and relieved. I was talking to myself as I left the place, when a moving shadow crept up behind me. The fragrance of jasmine followed me. This cursed marriage would not take place. The Dharma-shastra would be upheld.*

The Golden Cage

It was around noon. The mighty sun unleashed its tyrannical heat over the city. Its burning rays rolled down like balls of fire on the rare onlookers lurking around the deserted streets. Pondicherry wore its ghostly mask with the metallic sound of store shutters coming down in Nehru Street. Stray dogs that still had the energy to walk flocked along the canal, tongues hanging out, looking for food that people threw into round cement dustbins along the road. Kumar moved forward aimlessly on Komutti Street. He covered his face with the end of the *thundu* wrapped around his head. The stifling heat slowed him down as he approached one of the three streets that went around the Chetty Temple, inhabited by the Chettiar community.

Within a few days, Kumar's poor but peaceful life had become a living hell. His old parents, not wanting to be a burden, had killed themselves by consuming *datura*. The rest of the family had usurped the old shanty with its small piece of land on the pretext of covering an unpaid debt. They had then thrown him out of the community of potters. Kumar could have stayed in the village only if he had inherited his ancestral profession. But his father wanted him to have a better future by sending him to school instead of teaching him the trade. Kumar had been punished by his community because he was educated.

With no family, no work and no home, the young man joined the bandwagon of homeless people whose only purpose was to find a handful of rice and a place to sleep.

'Amma! A drop of water, please!' Just as she sat on the teak swing in the middle of the *thalvaram*, Kirtana heard a hesitant voice from the street. She put the *Kumudam* magazine on the swing hanging from the ceiling and went towards the kitchen. She stood on tiptoe to grab the glass meant 'for others'. Just as she turned towards the entrance, her mother came forward carrying a pot full of water.

'*Chi, chi! Po! Po!* This *thinnai* is not for people like you! Go somewhere else! We don't have any water!' screamed the mother, emptying the jug over the *thinnai*.

Kumar did not have time to react. The water touched his feet and flooded his dirty *kaili*. He jumped off the *thinnai* and ran away. He would have fallen off the footpath had he not gripped one of the wooden columns supporting the cemented tile roof. He was about to leave when a silhouette, accompanied by the sound of a *kolusu*, came forward.

'You are disgusting, Ma! You preferred wasting a whole jug of water on the *thinnai* to chase that man away instead of quenching his thirst with just a glass of water!' exclaimed Kirtana, looking at her mother angrily.

She went down the three small steps and gave the glass to the young man. Her mother charged down and snatched the glass from her daughter, putting it down noisily on the *thinnai*. Two or three drops of water spilled out of the aluminium glass and fell on the wet floor.

'If you want to give him water, put it on the ground. Since when have we started going close to these people?'

The mother and the daughter looked at each other defiantly, ignoring the presence of the poor young man who did not know what to do.

'Wait until your father comes. You don't listen to anybody! You do whatever you want!' mumbled her mother, going back into the house.

Kirtana watched her go. She made sure her mother was at a distance before holding out the glass to Kumar who looked embarrassed.

'It's all right. You can put it on the *thinnai*. I'll take it myself.'

The young girl pretended not to listen and came closer to him. Kumar bent over and took the glass in his hand. He then placed his right hand a few centimetres from his mouth, threw his head back, without touching the glass with his lips.

His Adam's apple went up and down to the rhythm of the water flowing down like a torrent. A small trickle went down his lips. Wiping his mouth, he gave the empty glass back to the young girl.

'Do you want some more?' asked Kirtana.

'Thank you. May God bless you!' he said, shaking his head to say no, hands folded in gratitude.

Kirtana took the glass. When she reached the entrance, she turned back towards the young man.

'If you are tired, you can rest on the backseat of the rickshaw,' she said, pointing towards the vehicle tied to one of the columns, and went back into the house without waiting for an answer.

Uncertain, the young man looked around. A few men and women sitting on the *thinnai* of the neighbouring houses looked at him with pity. A few were chatting, while others took a nap. They were servants who worked for the *ashramite*s for twelve to fifteen hours a day and were now resting.

'Since she has given you permission, why don't you go and sit on the rickshaw? You look tired. This Chettiar Amma does not have a heart. Go and rest,' said the old woman, stretching her legs out and chewing betel.

Kumar pulled up the hood of the rickshaw and sat on the bench. He closed his eyes. Images of the day flashed in his mind like a silent movie. Within minutes, he fell asleep. He had started his journey at dawn and had not slept at all the day before. The anguish of uncertainty had kept him awake all night. He would have wanted the night to be eternal. The fear of the future enveloped him like the dark.

At the break of dawn, he left the village and looked sadly at the hut where he had grown up one last time. He stopped for a moment at the potter's wheel abandoned by his father. The wheel – a symbol of eternal time and movement. As a child, he used to admire his father working on it, agile and graceful. Kumar would look at his father in admiration as objects took shape in his muddy hands, even as he was not allowed to learn this ancestral art. The poor potter often told his son: 'It's high time that our hands changed colour. For generations these hands reddened by clay should now discover the blue of ink. This chakra that our family has been turning for generations should stop with me. You should become a Chakravarti, my son!' Yes, the wheel had turned, but Kumar had not become a Chakravarti. He was a poor abandoned orphan whose life had been thrown into an infernal tornado.

A distant cousin in Kosapalayam had once told him that he could count on him in case of need. When he arrived at the bus station of Pondicherry, Kumar's head was full of dreams. But not for long. His embarrassed cousin had shattered all his hopes when the young man reached the hut in the potters' neighbourhood. 'I said that out of formality; I did not think that you would take it seriously. I already find it difficult to make ends meet with my wife and five children. What would I do with you? Moreover, you do not even know the trade!' he said, scratching his head, putting a crumpled ten rupee note in his pocket. Kumar left with a heavy heart and tears in his eyes.

He roamed around aimlessly in this strange city. On leaving Kosapalayam, he entered a large street teeming with people. At the crossroads of Raja Theatre intersection, he watched the traffic lights in admiration as pedestrians patiently waited for the colour to change. In spite of his sadness, he smiled inwardly at the power of this simple object, making so many unruly people obey. He entered Nehru Street and got lost in the crowd that was leaving the beautiful shops with flashy signboards. The clock of the Grand Bazaar rang ten times, and the market was bubbling with activity. He was used to the silence of his small village and felt drowned by the noise of horns of cars, motorcycles and tempos. Bicycles zig-zagged between people. Cows, pigs, dogs and beggars fought around dustbins. When he reached Gandhi Street, he came across the sight of a bullock cart blocking traffic. The two bullocks, beaten by the heat and fatigue, refused to go further. Trucks and cars blew their horns frenetically. Enraged, the cart puller let the bullocks loose, who charged straight into the crowd. People dispersed and fled in all directions. The policeman dressed in white with a red *kepi* was exhausted and beyond himself. He accosted the cart puller who was running behind his bullocks.

Kumar felt as if he was crossing an invisible door as he went over the canal in the White Town. Another world opened in front of him. 'If Brahma is quiet, this must be his kingdom,' he said to himself, going past VAK, a bookshop of spiritual literature. 'And this God has power over noise. By what magic does the noise stop after the canal?' Lost in thought, he stopped before the Ganesha temple and prayed, his eyes closed. He looked to the right; it seemed as if the street stopped at the imposing Cercle de Pondichéry, whereas it went much further. Kumar decided to take a left where strangely dressed mild-mannered people with discreet manners were moving towards a grey and white building. He followed them and reached the Samadhi of Sri Aurobindo. The austerity of this neighbourhood and its inhabitants was in sharp contrast to the Black Town. A disturbing and respectful silence reigned over the place.

Kumar was shocked by the people's clothes. For the most part, the men were wearing long shirts that went to their knees, matched with flared pants in immaculate white. Some were wearing khaki shorts with white shirts. The women looked like the Kanchanas and Saroja Devis he saw in films. They were wearing tight long robes that hugged their bodies and balloon pants. The only difference was that their clothes were coloured and they were wearing shawls over their shoulders. The sight of the shawl made the young man want to draw a moustache on his face, wear a wig that would put to shame all the wig wearers of the world and clothes that no designer could conjure up in their dreams. He would then do crazy things while pulling away the shawls of these women. In this part of the world, Kama, while intoxicated one day, said that seduction should start by teasing. In other places, one seduced by using the mind, bravery or romance; here, it was clownery, where actors resembling big pink sweets seduced actresses by pulling their hair, by strangling them with shawls and throwing them over. They played hide-and-seek behind cardboard sculptures, making them fall and roll on dirty grass and finally threw them in multi-coloured fountains.

Kumar looked around him. There was no grass, no park, no fountain. He left the place under the strict stare of an old *ashramite* sitting at the entrance. He must have read his thoughts. After all, weren't they all yogis? He went along the samadhi and turned right. At the end of Rue François Martin he came upon the park of the Governor's Palace. His face lit up. 'There is a real park here! Grass, sculptures and a fountain!' he said to himself, looking sadly at a young *ashramite* disappearing into a canteen at the side of the patisserie. He crossed the park and reached another part of the town which was even more surprising.

The streets were broad with beautiful cream and yellow villas from where frangipani and bougainvillea shrubs sprung out. His mind was confused as he tried to read the names of the streets that were impossible to pronounce. Compared to the houses in the Tamil town, here the doors were closed and the neighbourhood was almost empty. The few people he came across had light skin; others, dressed in European clothes, had white skin. Even if it was difficult to make eye contact because of their straw hats, he felt a little disdain. '*Aiyo vellakaran!*' he murmured. He hurried to leave the neighbourhood, feeling like a complete stranger. Feeling more at ease in the Black Town, he decided to go back to people who looked like him.

Kumar made the young *ashramite* roll on the grass which smelt a bit strange. Hands on his hips, he watched her go down the little slope at the end of the park. He would have wanted her to go as far as Nandi's basin, but the young girl who had had enough of rolling stopped in front of the small fountain with the statue of a woman pouring water from an earthen pot. He jumped around her with hands behind his back, like the popular actor MGR.

He gripped the scarf, tied it around his hip and made the young girl spin like a top: '*Appit!*' he cried out. Then, he took her in his arms and threw her in the fountain. Some drops of water splashed on his yellow and orange suit as he hid his face in the young woman's neck and closed his eyes.

'Ah, we finally found a rickshaw driver!' A man's voice shook him out of his romantic dream. The neck where he had put his face was just the rod of the rickshaw's hood. Surprised, he realized that he was still sitting on the bench of the vehicle. An old man was washing his feet on the first step of the house. The young lady he had met before was standing by his side, folding his umbrella.

'No, Papa. It was a passerby; he was tired. I gave him permission to rest on the rickshaw,' answered the girl in a low voice. 'Of course, Ma did not like it and tried to chase him away. But a *thinnai* is also meant to give shelter to travellers, isn't it?'

'Of course,' said the man, touched by his daughter's generosity. 'But, you know your mother, don't you?'

He turned to Kumar and called him.

'Hey you, come here!'

'Yes, sir.'

The young man hurriedly got off the rickshaw and came close to the Chettiar. In a few sentences, Kumar explained his situation to him. The Chettiar looked at him from top to bottom, and satisfied, asked him, 'If you are looking for work, I can give it to you. You can ride the rickshaw if you like. All you have to do is take my daughter to dance classes. That's all. *C'est tout. Tu seras payé, nourri et tu peux dormir sur le thinnai à l'arrière de la maison.*' (You will be paid and you can sleep on the *thinnai* behind the house. I will also give you food.)

Kumar scratched his head. His gaze went from the rickshaw to the Chettiar and his fingers rolled around the *thundu* under his right arm.

'It's just that… I am educated, sir,' he said, hesitating.

'So what? Do you think you can become a manager in my shop?' The Chettiar's voice rose in irritation and became threatening. 'Listen, I don't have time to waste. It is this, or nothing. If you are not interested in my proposal, you can get lost!'

Without waiting for an answer, the Chettiar climbed up the stairs and disappeared into the house.

For the first time, Kumar looked at the young girl. She was a ravishing beauty. She looked like the drawings of Maruthi women published in *Ananda Vikatan*, the Tamil magazine. Her round face and light skin were beautiful. Her long and thick lashes were like stormy clouds covering big expressive black eyes. Her delicate nose and fleshy lips gave her a joyous look. Her curly hair tied in braids by a *sungu* went down to her hips. And when she moved, she left behind a delicate fragrance and the tinkling music of *kolusu*. Kumar was struck motionless by her beauty. He could not take his eyes off the young girl, who smiled back at him. She almost looked mysterious. It seemed as if she wanted him to stay and take the job that her father had offered.

From a young age, Kirtana felt like a stranger in her milieu. Since she was small, her frail shoulders carried the weight of her demanding parents' hopes and stifling love, obsessed by the purity of their caste. They wanted Kirtana to set an example, especially her obsessive and tyrannical mother. They had turned their daughter into a knowledgeable monkey who knew how to dance, play the veena and sing Carnatic vocals. Her father showed her off in front of guests and said that Bhima and Nala were novices compared to Kirtana when it came to cooking. They were raising her to become a good wife, a good mother and a good homemaker. But Kirtana had other ambitions. She dreamt of adventures and romance. Her role models were Lakshmi Sahgal, Kadambini Ganguly, Homai Vyarawalla, Durba Banerjee and all the women who rejected orthodox values and patriarchy. This paradoxical society worshipped imaginary women in temples but shut them in kitchens in reality. Kirtana refused to be a part of it. Her parents knew her strength of character and had only one ambition: to marry her off as soon as possible to curb her romantic enthusiasm.

The wheel kept on turning in Kumar's favour. His life had changed ever since he came to the Chettiar's home. After a while, he had become the Chettiar's right-hand man. No more rickshaw! No more sleeping on the *thinnai*! The Chettiar had bought him a bicycle and even given him a small room at the back of the house. Much to the dislike of Chettiar Amma, who nonetheless appreciated the handyman qualities of a jack of all trades at which Kumar excelled.

On that day, the young man was present on all fronts. At dawn, he woke up the old servant, Saroja, to draw the *kolam*, then went to the Grand Bazaar to buy flowers, fruits, sweets and all types of vegetables to feed the people coming to the house. It was the day of the 'ceremony to see the girl', which was all about the first meeting between the future husband and wife. The previous day, the Chettiar had given him all the orders, and Kumar wanted to show him that he was capable of carrying them out. He was doubly attentive and ran around getting everything done. One instant, he was in the kitchen watching over the brahmin cook hired for the occasion, and the next, he was making sure the driver had cleaned the car properly and was ready to welcome the visitors at the station. He hurried towards the backyard where Saroja and another servant were busy washing banana leaves near the well. He examined the leaves one by one and the bronze utensils too. Not satisfied with the way the glasses were cleaned, he showed the servant how to clean them with tamarind. Then, folding his *kaili*, he went to inspect the toilets. He yelled at the servants who were dusting old photos hanging on the *thalvaram*, shining under the glass lamp. Losing his temper, he grabbed the duster from one of the servants and started cleaning the beautiful chandelier of Venetian crystal. When he got off the stool, he felt Kirtana's questioning gaze upon him. All day long, he ran around, avoiding this gaze. Kirtana was silently accusing him of participating in this masquerade. She had secretly nursed a love for him from the moment she saw him sitting on the backseat of the rickshaw like an injured bird, vulnerable, impoverished and lost in this strange city. She had liked his fragility, his humility, but also his will to survive. He could have gone and joined the queue of beggars and homeless people, but he chose to fight against this unfair life. It was this audacity and courage that she liked about him.

The day had been long. Kumar could not get any sleep. Hands behind his neck, he gazed at the ceiling. His empty head was crowded by images of the day. Everyone was happy, especially Chettiar Amma. Before leaving, the *tharagar* took her aside and told her the marriage was secretly confirmed. Brimming with joy, she stuffed the crisp new notes in the folds of his *veshti*, spitting out betel juice in the bronze spittoon. The Chettiar had spent the whole day showing off his Tanjore paintings, his Burma teak pillars and the Venetian chandelier. His wife had to intervene when he started talking about his great family that had built the Mariamman Temple in Saigon. She changed the topic when he began talking about the adventures of the Nattukottai Chettiars, his ancestors; how they had travelled across the seas and made a fortune in Indochina. In all the bonhomie, nobody noticed Kirtana's sadness, neither the tears that had run down the chords of her veena strings when she started the *charanam* of Nagumomu Ganaleni. Even Thyagaraja would not have understood that this song of distress was meant not for Nagaraja, but for Kumar. The young man closed his eyes and fell into deep sleep.

The sound of the door opening woke him up. A shadow came up from behind and entered the dark room. He wanted to get up and turn on the light.

'No, don't switch on the light,' whispered a stifled voice.

A firm but soft hand touched his shoulder.

'Come, let's go!'

Marguerite

Marguerite's looks were fixed on the still body of her husband soaked in blood. Her right hand was still trembling. Blood drops fell from the *aruvamanai* in pollock patterns on the black-and-white tiles she hated so much. She had always complained about them and wanted to change the chequered floor in the suburban apartment. No luck. The dirty and ugly flooring had irked her ever since she was a child. Due to a lack of money, her old father had never given in to her demands. By the time Marguerite inherited the apartment, she had no energy left. It felt like a bad game of chess in which she had lost her entire existence. Ironically, she was the one who was called rani but was treated like an ordinary pawn all her life.

She jumped when the phone rang. Who was it? She had forgotten that she had dialled the police, but had hung up, feeling scared of the persistent ringing. She used the tip of her sari to hold the black handset which was slippery with the blood on her hand.

'Hello! You had called the police station, but the call was disconnected. How can we help you? What is your name?'

Marguerite was trembling and did not know what to say. She mustered the courage and murmured in a barely audible voice.

'Marguerite Sept-Montagnes.'

'Pardon me? Can you please repeat?'

'Marguerite Sept-Montagnes,' she murmured.

'Sept-Montagnes. Seven like the number and montagnes like… mountains?'

Marguerite hesitated. Fear replaced shame. She put the phone down abruptly.

Sept-Montagnes. She hated her family name! Like an invisible leper, she was ashamed of her ridiculous name since childhood. She had never gotten used to this patronym whose history had been victoriously narrated by the family.

On an evening in 1881, Daniel Sept-Montagnes's great grandfather did something that would have serious consequences on this poor family of pariahs. On the night of 4 August 1881 to be precise, there was a big party at Louis Rassendren's house.

This aristocrat was from the caste of Vellalas and was getting ready to celebrate a historic day.

The decree of renunciation, for which he and his friends had fought for many years, was going to finally be signed by Jules Grévy. The house on Vellala Street was brimming with activity. Everybody was giving finishing touches under the strict supervision of the master of ceremonies who was trying to hide his worries. He was troubled because his friend and companion Ponnuthambi Pillai was about to arrive any minute, and the damned pariahs had not yet reached! It was his bright idea to invite the pariahs for dinner. When the neighbours heard of it, they protested in front of Louis Rassendren's house. But Ponnuthambi Pillai did not budge. He absolutely wanted to exhibit democratic ways by saying no to casteist behaviour.

He would also invite all the pariahs in town and the neighbouring villages to come for a community meal with him. But unfortunately, nobody dared venture on this street, which had been out of bounds for them for centuries. When Ponnuthambi Pillai reached, he was surprised and disappointed to see that there was nobody there. After talking to his friend Rassendren and the other people gathered around for the occasion, he was about to cancel the dinner when Ezhumalai, Daniel's great grandfather, arrived. With hands folded behind his back, the man looked around the house nonchalantly, glancing at the pictures hanging on the wall.

He ignored the men staring at him. After finishing his inspection, Ezhumalai sat down in all his Pondicherrian glory.

Nicely settled in his chair, he unfolded the extensions on the handrest, putting his feet on them insolently, waiting to be served.

Ezhumalai was born insolent! The eldest son in a family of many, he never had to do anything in his life. He refused to work in the fields on the pretext of having been educated by white missionaries. But in reality, the man did not know how to read or write. Out of ambition, his father sent him to the priest at the church of Saint Andrew of Reddiarpalayam, who, apart from serving at the church, used to educate children from the neighbouring villages. He had started the seminar of Arikamedu where missionaries propagated the message of Christ in Molière's language. They also welcomed all the children coming to this modest school with open arms. This was neither out of love for the Catholic religion nor this language that Ezhumalai's father could not understand. Very soon his faulty enthusiasm died in front of Ezhumalai, who was stretching his limits. Ezhumalai had only learnt the rudiments of French which was enough to pass him off as a scholar. Since he was an insolent troublemaker, to maintain peace the villagers named him Nattamai. As the village chief, he did not mean harm to anyone. So, when he heard about the community meal to celebrate the decree of renunciation, he put on his best attire and reached Louis Rassendren's house as a representative of the pariahs.

In spite of a heated discussion, the man did not utter a word over dinner. He casually listened to his hosts, enjoying the unawaited feast. Bloated with the success of the decree of renunciation, Ponnuthambi Pillai and his friends burnt the old society down with their words, wishing it the end. Ezhumalai did not understand anything. Bored with the conversation, he decided to leave, but stopped when Ponnuthambi Pillai declared his historic decision in a serious voice.

'I have made my decision, friends. I have decided to give up my customs. From a French subject, I would like to become a French citizen under the empire of French law. I have thus decided to give up my caste name Pillai. From today onwards, I would like to be called La Porte. This symbolic name that I have decided to take opens the door to a better future for my brothers and sisters from lower castes who have been oppressed for centuries. From now on, my only mission would be to defend the most underprivileged.' He stopped, satisfied with his speech and glanced questioningly at his companions. Taken aback, they did not quite know how to react to this decision. Embracing the republican values of the colonizer was one thing; but rejecting the system was quite another. Ponnuthambi Pillai was far from giving up his caste name. For centuries they had been mistreated and rejected by the higher castes. The arrival of French people had changed their destinies.

They now belonged to a new elite created recently by colonization. Given the same status as traditional upper castes, they rejoiced as privileged people for two centuries. Giving up everything to be on the same level as the pariahs was unthinkable. Taking advantage of the silence, Ezhumalai got up and said to Ponnuthambi Pillai.

'What does La Porte mean?' His tone was insolent.

'La Porte? A door, what else?!'

'What, a door? As in… *kadhavu*?

'Yes, *kadhavu* in Tamil and *porte* in French.'

Ponnuthambi Pillai looked a bit annoyed.

'You haven't understood the explanation?'

'Yes, but it is funny to choose such an insignificant name.'

Irritated by the rude comment, Ponnuthambi Pillai raised his voice, 'Ah yes? After everything I just said, you find the name insignificant?'

'I think, yes.'

Ezhumalai put his little finger in his right ear and rubbed hard.

'Now that we are talking about it, I also want to renounce.'

'Good idea! But this is not the townhall. In any case, we have to wait for a few months for the law to be implemented. You have all the time you need to think about it.'

Feeling seriously challenged, Ponnuthambi Pillai turned towards his friend, looking at him furiously. Louis Rassendren was feeling uncomfortable and tried to push Ezhumalai towards the door. No luck. Ezhumalai refused to budge.

'Since you…' He stopped, starting again. 'Since you have chosen a French name, give me one also!'

Ezhumalai's request was met with an embarrassing silence. He went to the group and throwing his *thundu* over his shoulder, said, 'Since Ponnuthambi Pillai has chosen La Porte as his patronym, I will change mine to Fenêtre!' As the guests left discreetly, Ponnuthambi Pillai was still, watching the confronted one leave in sadness and anger.

A few months later, all of Pondicherry would recall Ezhumalai's act of renunciation. The village cock lost his feathers when Ezhumalai left his village early. Scared that the cock would wake up the entourage and that his neighbours would reach the townhall before him, Ezhumalai tried to catch it before he crowed. But the sly bird escaped from his hands and ran down the alley like a headless chicken, crying out stridently in a cloud of feathers. The entire village woke up.

When he reached the townhall, surrounded by an unruly crowd, Ezhumalai was in a strident mood. He would have liked to be the first one to renounce in the village. All the way from Uzhavarkarai to the town, he was taken aback by questions he did not know how to answer.

The Renunciation. Apart from the new elite of the Vellalas, the rest of the population had no idea what this meant. Some thought that from then onwards, they would have the same rights as white people and that they could dress like them. Others pretended that they would become French citizens, leave their country and go to France. A fair amount of people started talking about this among themselves.

When his turn came, Ezhumalai looked at the government employee high-headedly, as if the latter was the fool of the village.

'Name?' asked the employee without looking at him.

'Ezhumalai.'

'Profession?'

'None.'

'Caste?'

'Mudaliar.' The employee frowned without looking at Ezhumalai.

'Have you chosen a name?'

'Yes, Fenêtre.'

'What? Fenêtre?' The employee lifted his head up for the first time. He looked straight at the averagely tall man who was well dressed. His hair was well brushed; his shirt and immaculately white *veshti* was a class apart from the other candidates. Compared to most of the aspirants before him, a certain assurance emanated from this individual, who was standing confidently. The employee put his pen down on the table and looked him straight in the eye.

'And may I know why Fenêtre? Why not Terrasse, Pilier or Chambre?' he asked, teasingly.

'Why not? Ponnuthambi Pillai chose La Porte!' he said defiantly.

'Ah yes, I understand now. Ponnuthambi Pillai had a reason for choosing this name. What is yours?'

'I don't have one. I don't think that should be a reason for renunciation.'

The employee looked a little amused and broke the familiarity. He took on a serious air and started looking at his files again.

'No, I cannot accept this. Choose another name and hurry up! There are other people waiting.'

Ezhumalai lost his confidence and seemed disappointed. Not knowing what to do, he turned towards his companions who could not understand what was going on. They could not do anything to help. As he turned, his gaze fell upon a portrait hanging on the wall. He looked at the picture and asked, 'Who is this?'

Surprised by the question, the employee turned mechanically towards the wall.

'That is Napoléon the Emperor!' His hesitant voice, expected the worst.

'Give me his name then, Emperor Napoléon.' He turned sideways, and like the emperor put his right hand on his abdomen. Two minutes later, he was on the footpath of the Barracks of the Sepoys, the back of his *veshti* marked by the footprint of the employee.

The 'mission civilisatrice' was unfolding in an alarming way!

His self-respect lost, Ezhumalai left the place without asking for anything more. He joined the others and left for his village, promising that nobody would renounce. Luck was on his side. On the pretext of bad behaviour, he made sure that nobody became French apart from himself. This is how Ezhumalai Sept-Montagnes and his family became the only French citizens in the village.

Daniel, Ezhumalai's great grandson, was among the thousands of people that the colonial machine had worked against. Among his family, he was the one who should have lived in France. His grandfather's arrogance and his father's ignorance had played an important part in determining his destiny since 1881.

From 16 August 1962 to 15 February 1963, the old trade post was swept by a tornado of confusion. During this period, the inhabitants of Pondicherry could choose to remain French or become citizens of the new Indian nation. The renouncers did not know if they would be affected by this law. People living in French territories, who had become French by choice, were clueless about what to do after de Gaulle's declaration. And finally, others opted for citizenship without knowing what was in store for them with this new status.

Daniel's father was among the first category. Considering himself French, he did not think that he would have to choose. When his cousins invited him to join them and put his name on the list of people opting for French citizenship, he accused them of being jealous and playing tricks on him to take revenge and refused to go into town. In spite of the encouragement from others, he did nothing about it and did not take the news seriously. What was he going to do with the citizenship of a country he did not know? The new Indian nation would restore his pride. To hell with the *vellakarans*! The piece of land he had inherited from his father was enough to feed his small family. Eighty-two years after the renunciation, the Sept-Montagnes family kept its name but lost citizenship.

Years went by, while Daniel's family became poorer, families that chose France went to the metropolis to make a living. They became rich and came back to live in the beautiful neighbourhoods of Pondicherry. Abandoning their land and struck by poverty, Daniel's parents took refuge with the nouveau riche. They became servants and their life was a struggle. The only way out was to become French. Patiently and tediously, Daniel's father spent years trying to regain French citizenship. This did not stop him from raising his son with the fantasy of a nation he did not know. The Tamil dreams of the young boy were perfumed with eau de cologne and savon de Marseille. For entertainment, the emperor of a kingdom of chocolate saw himself sitting on a mountain of sweets. Draped in the silver foil of Poulain chocolate, he reigned over an army of centurions in the armour of canned food that his cousins brought when they came home. He was the descendant of people who had drunk the magic potion, not speaking Gaulish, not knowing who was a Roman and who was a Gaul. All that he dreamt of was to live like his cousins, to talk like them and to dress like them. And most of all, to shrug his shoulders like them. But nothing changed. The legal procedure was taking long. The uncertainty was not good for his disoriented life. He had stopped studying French at the Alliance Française in the hope of leaving for his Eldorado. The young man put his destiny in the hands of time while he melted in the doldrums of Pondicherry.

Tired of waiting, his father married him off to a girl from the village, and after paying a *bakshish* got him a job at the Public Works Department. Daniel did not understand his job. Being incompetent and unqualified, his boss gave him menial tasks like cleaning the canal of Pondicherry. Completed in 1788, the canal divides the town into two according to a system of apartheid peculiar to colonization. White people on one side and Indians on the other. It was a beautiful little river all the same. It was used for public toilets and dumping waste, as if the Black Town threw all its dirt there to take revenge for three centuries of colonization. His childhood dreams melted into the canal which flowed into the sea near Dubrayapet, in an imaginary no man's land where the dreamland and native land merged into one eternally. Since France was making him wait, he made the desired land enter his heart and his mannerisms. Without knowing who he was, one could think that he was a retired soldier. It so happened that even Franco-Pondicherrians on holidays took him for one of their own – so confusing were his clothes and mannerisms. His wardrobe had Tahiti shirts, tee shirts of different military regiments, fake Polo and Lacoste tee shirts from Barbes. He had become so French that his colleagues teased him and called him '*soldat mestry*'. No amount of ragging could make him deviate from his ambition.

Daniel let his tears flow when flight AI 320 took off from the Meenambakkam Airport. The ride from Pondicherry to Madras was a delicious ordeal. Torn between reaching the land of his dreams and the sadness of leaving his family behind, he was in complete disarray. The smile of his daughter, Marguerite, had snatched the joy of his victory against destiny. All he needed was an old document of renunciation and a false birth certificate to throw his life into uncertainty.

Marguerite was five years old when she reached France. Her father had a stable job, a decent salary and a modest apartment in Sarcelles. He had worked hard. Saving every dime, he accepted all kinds of jobs and his patience paid off. A kind old lady for whom he did housekeeping, found him a job in a hospital where her son worked. Daniel, the '*soldat mestry*', became a maintenance officer at the hospital of Gonesse and shifted from the Sonacotra where he was living with a friend.

Being the only daughter, Marguerite was showered with love and raised like a princess. The sweet young girl was a good student. She was quickly noticed by her teachers who promised her a bright future. Her life would have been perfect if that disaster in the summer of 1985 had not happened.

As usual, their holidays in Pondicherry were boring and tiresome. It was always the same people with awkward, shy smiles who came home to take their gifts. It was the unavoidable trip to Velankanni that Marguerite hated the most. She hated everything about the excursion. Packed like a tin of sardines in the old bus, the family embarked on a boring ride, smelling of cod and tamarind rice kept in the back for the lunch break. Velankanni was the place of pilgrimage, noisy and crowded with no place to eat or stay. She was repulsed by everything on this trip. While her parents made their way through the crowd for the mass, the young girl stayed behind with a family member who was dreaming of palaces in Jaipur and the Taj Mahal.

The only palace she knew was the Halwa Mahal where the family stopped for the famous sweets of Karaikal. During her holidays, Marguerite waited for one single thing: to go back. The return could have been sooner, if only her older aunt had not arrived that evening. Angry with her brother for a long time, Daniel's sister never came during the vacations. Everyone was surprised when she got off the rickshaw and entered the family home without greeting anyone. When she discovered that Daniel had gone out to do some errands, she took a chair and sat down in the middle of the *maada kudam* in a dark silence.

When Daniel stopped in front of the house, there was panic. He recognised his sister's rickshaw driver and greeted her warmly. '*Ennacka*? When did you reach?' he asked, taking his shoes off. Trying to sound as natural as possible, he seemed suspicious. He came closer to her and kissed her on both cheeks. Without moving from her chair, his sister gave him a fake hug. There was something terribly wrong. He also pulled a chair, looking in despair at his wife who was packing. She did not know how to react. A few minutes ago, she had walked up to her sister-in-law to wish her. Greeted by an unfriendly and severe look, she retired to her room, feeling distrustful.

The sister broke the uncomfortable silence, like an unwanted guest in the room, and suddenly asked, 'Where is your daughter?'

'Wait, *Acka*, I will go and see.'

Relieved on finding an excuse to leave, Daniel got up and went to the room. He left the shopping bags near his wife, looking at her questioningly. Not getting a reply, he went back and sat down.

'Marguerite has gone out with her cousins, *Acka*,' he said. 'They must have gone for a walk to the Cours Chabrol. Is there any particular reason why you are asking after her?'

He asked the question carefully, not wanting to bother his sister.

'Can't a mother-in-law ask about her daughter-in-law?'

The question struck like lightning. It echoed in Daniel's ears. Panic-stricken, he turned towards his wife for an answer. She dropped her bags and went closer to the bedroom door.

'What... What are you trying to say, *Acka*?' asked Daniel, his voice trembling. He was expecting the worst.

'Have you forgotten your promise, *Thambi*?

His sister was savouring every word. She had been waiting for this moment for a long time.

'Do you really want me to remind you?'

The question fell like an axe. Daniel froze. Not mustering enough courage to stop his sister from leaving, he looked at his devastated family.

When she realised that her childhood dream of becoming a doctor had been destroyed, Marguerite was torn apart. Not only was she being forced to get married, but the family also wanted to stop her studies. She had tried her best to make her father change his mind, but to no avail. Since that terrible evening, Daniel was like the living dead. The promise made in the euphoria of leaving and the sadness of being far crushed the happiness of his beloved daughter. Daniel still kept holding strong, but he had to give in eventually under pressure from all the others. Faced with such blackmail, he had no other option but to sacrifice his daughter's happiness.

Selvam joined his wife one year after marriage. In between, Marguerite found a job as a receptionist at the Préfecture of Enghien-les-Bains and started her new unwanted life with apprehension. This marriage was not meant to be since the beginning, because the couple was diametrically opposed. Marguerite was soft and intelligent; Selvam was rustic and rough. He had no savoir-vivre... He just did not know how to live. Strangely, the young man's life resembled his uncle and father-in-law Daniel's life. Like him, he grew up with a French dream, with the promise of marrying Marguerite. What was the use of studying in India when the French Eldorado was on the horizon?

In spite of difficult beginnings, their life took a nice turn on the birth of their daughter. Selvam found a regular job in a museum as a nightguard and even planned to move out to start a new family life. But Daniel was against this. He wanted the couple to be more stable financially before they lived on their own. He was actually afraid of letting Marguerite go. He dreaded that moment when he would have to live alone with his wife for the rest of his life. Scared of Selvam's immaturity and his daughter's lack of experience, he wanted to play it safe before letting them go. But this proved to be disastrous.

Marguerite's life plunged into darkness after her parents left home and retired in Pondicherry. They abandoned their daughter with the deprived monster that Selvam had become. He was slowly devouring their daughter and granddaughter. Afraid of family dishonour, they turned a deaf ear when Marguerite talked about her bad luck. Not a single day went by when Selvam did not come home drunk or drugged to beat up the two victims.

Alcohol, drugs and gambling took over Selvam's life. He lost his job, dignity and common sense. Caught in the avalanche of misfortune, Marguerite thought about leaving her husband many a time. But family blackmail left her vulnerable and helpless. She gave up and lived through this ordeal until that fatal day.

On a winter evening, Marguerite and her daughter were surprised to find Selvam back home earlier than usual. He was drunk, his eyes were bloodshot. He had hardly stepped in when he asked Marguerite for money. She refused to give him any. She carefully saved her money for year-end celebrations. She was determined not to give him any, even if it meant having a bad time. Her daughter hid in her room when she heard a ghastly slap.

Usually, Selvam banged the door and left, calling her all kinds of names. But that evening, she heard footsteps in the living room. Marguerite's sobs were lost in the noise of Selvam opening and closing drawers. She heard him go towards the kitchen where Marguerite hid her money in the spice box.

A container of chili powder fell on the black-and-white tiled floor, the red powder smeared across the floor. Sneezing and coughing, Selvam cursed the gods. Horrified, the young girl opened the door softly to see what was going on. But the door, which had not been greased, opened with a creak, grabbing her father's attention.

She hardly had time to react; he was already on the threshold, blocking the door with his foot.

Marguerite turned when she heard her daughter scream. Something strange was happening in her room. The door was closed.

'Amma!' The adolescent's voice resonated like lightning in the whole apartment.

Marguerite ran into the kitchen. She slipped on the chilli powder and hit herself against the kitchen sink. A bit stunned, she managed to get up and began looking for something. Her eyes fell upon the *aruvamanai* that she had used to scale the fish with.

She bent over her daughter's naked body. The *aruvamanai* with which she had stabbed Selvam on the back looked like a question mark between life and death.

The Postman, the Madman and the Drunkard

Kousalya supraja Rama poorva sandhya pravarthathe... The first shlokas of *Suprabhatam* rang out from the Perumal Kovil. Eyes closed, Pattabhiram had waited in fear for the sacred chants. He so wanted that tiresome and sleepless night to come to an end. Disturbed by the barking of street dogs and the snoring of the vagabond sleeping on the neighbour's *thinnai*, the old man had not slept a wink. He had prayed to all the gods, especially to Kaal Bhairav to stop time. The dreaded day was finally dawning. In spite of the January morning chill, drops of sweat appeared on his back and on his forehead. He stood up, adjusted the sacred thread hanging on his torso and sat down on the mat. He took the *thundu* lying on his side and wiped himself without opening his eyes.

Since his younger days, he had this habit of not opening his eyes to anything unfortunate that could transform into a devastating day. His ritual was to slide his two palms down his face, from the forehead to the chin, covering his eyes. After a few moments of silence, he rubbed his palms against each other, finally opening his eyes to study the lines on his hands. Then, listening to the sacred chants, he meditated. The day could then begin.

The pious old postman was driven by an unshakeable faith. His whole being exuded spirituality. His soft words, immaculate clothes, harmonious gestures and gentle smile attracted everyone and they held him in high esteem. It had been almost forty years since he had been scouring the streets of Pondicherry. Pattabhiram knew all the neighbourhoods like the back of his hand. Years of delivering letters had made him an important person in town. Everyone liked him, except his seniors. Pattabhiram was slow, but his lack of vivaciousness was not indolence. Not in the least!

Religious zeal and a talkative nature were the old postman's worst enemies. He could not go past a temple without stopping to pray. And God knows there were as many temples as bars in the small town! One would almost be led to believe that the number of temples reflected the religious fervour of the town. But the reality was that in the fragmented society every community had its own temple. There was a time when Shaivites did not want Vaishnavites in their temple. Those who were of the right-handed path did not want to share the same space with those of the left-handed path. The Mudaliars did not want the Chettiars, who did not want the pariahs who were converting to Catholicism to escape their destiny. The whites did not want the Malabars in the parish of Our Lady of Angels Church. The catholic Vellalars from the Immaculate Conception Cathedral refused to share space with the sub-castes, who ended up going to the Basilica of the Sacred Heart of Jesus built along the railway track.

Apart from the White Town, the Muslim quarters and the Centrale neighbourhood, every street had a place of worship, much to Pattabhiram's delight. He clearly preferred these neighbourhoods to others. Nobody complained about the old postman. Who would want to criticise such a religious man? However, something untowardly was going to disturb his peaceful existence. His previous boss, a man who was older than Pattabhiram and on the verge of retirement, had summoned the postman to his office a few days before leaving.

'Pattabhi, I have known you for a long time, a very long time indeed. Thirty years? Forty years?' asked the boss.

'Forty years, sir!' The old postman answered, proud of his memory.

'Forty years! *Ishvara*! Time flies.' He reached out for a file, but changed his mind and rang the bell. 'Bring two teas and some samosas!' he ordered. 'Give me that file,' he said, pointing towards a cardboard cover within arm's reach.

The old postman kept standing, not knowing what he was doing there. To avoid his boss's gaze, he pretended to look around the office that he otherwise knew well. On seeing pictures of Lord Ganesha hanging behind the boss's table, he closed his eyes and prayed for a few seconds.

'Have some tea, Pattabhi. Take some samosas also,' said the boss. The postman sat on the edge of the chair, looking petrified and a bit disturbed.

'Come on, no need to be formal! You know me well.' The boss pushed the cup of tea towards the postman, encouraging him with a gesture of the chin.

Certainly, the two men knew each other well.

Pattabhiram often came to his office to chat, but that was after work. In fact, the two men shared their passion for religion. Sometimes they would spend evenings together discussing the Puranas, the Vedas, the Upanishads and other holy scriptures. Sometimes they would get carried away by their fervour and get into philosophical discussions on deeper subjects like *Advaita*, *Samkhya*, etc. The director liked chatting with the old postman and admired his erudition on divine mysteries as well as human nature.

Forty years of distributing letters in all the corners of the town and his mania for chatting made him an expert on society, comparable to any sociologist. Who would imagine that a simple postman who spent his life distributing letters had developed such a sharp sense of analysis to understand this city?

'You see, Pattabhi,' said the boss, sipping his tea. 'I am sad to leave this place where I spent such a long time of my life. Do you remember the old post office?'

'Of course, sir!' answered Pattabhi, excited at the idea of talking about old memories. He was so scared that the boss had called him to scold him. 'I remember you as a young man, arriving from Trichy. It is thanks to you that the three counters that we called La Poste at that time were brought together in this beautiful building. You installed these telephone cabins outside with all the facilities. Without you, I would not dare imagine what would become of us!'

'I know, Pattabhi, I know.' The boss was lost for a moment in a cloud of vanity.

His face changed with pride and an arrogant and victorious smile spread across his face. It was true that without divine intervention La Poste would have remained as it was: three dirty, dingy rooms with employees hiding behind dusty piles of files and furniture. The old bureaucrat had battled hard with the chief minister to improve the working conditions and get a new modern building. The old building at the crossroads of Quai de Gingy and Ranga Pillai Street extended up to the end of Manakula Vinayagar. Even though this had no impact on the life of the old postman who spent all his time on the streets of Pondicherry, he was proud of going to the new building every morning.

'However, I am not interested in talking to you about myself, Pattabhi. I am worried about you. I am actually very concerned.'

'About me?' cried out the old postman. His voice echoed in an exaggerated manner along with the buzzing of the old air conditioner. Feeling ridiculous for having uttered that cry, Pattabhi apologised profusely and drank his tea.

'Yes, Pattabhi. Soon the new boss will take over, and he is young and unkind. He wants to change everything and modernise everything. He reminds me of me in my youth. He is right, this office is too old now. We are in competition with other companies that have modern tools. Soon there will be no need for postmen.'

'What? No more postmen?' Pattabhi jumped from his chair. 'But what are you trying to say? How will we live without postmen? Who will distribute the letters? How is this possible?' Panic spread across the old postman's face.

'My God, everything is possible, Pattabhi! You know that we are living in the Kali yuga. You see this machine? It is called a computer and people communicate by using this machine. We will not need letters, papers and stamps anymore.'

The old postman looked at the strange machine in awe. There was a screen and a keyboard. He had seen it several times in the office but had never tried to understand what it was used for. He thought it was one of the gadgets the boss enjoyed playing around with. He would never have imagined that this machine would be the end of postmen.

'But I don't understand, sir.' He was now panicking and began walking around the computer.

'Look Pattabhi.' The boss switched on the screen. 'Can you see this? It is called an e-mail. You type your message and the address of your correspondent, then you just have to press this send button. A second later, the person receives the message, no matter where they are in the world.' He was almost ashamed of showing Pattabhi how easy it had become to communicate without help from a tired old postman.

'I still don't understand who is going to send the message.' The old man's voice was irritated, and he was tearing up. He was under the impression that his boss was making fun of him. Was he being humiliated because of the last discussion on *Advaita*? A few weeks earlier, Pattabhi had beaten the boss with irrefutable arguments on the theory of non-duality. He was a fervent disciple of Sankara and Ramana Maharishi, and he was convinced that there was no separation between a subject and an object.

'Maybe you should spend more time on real things, instead of mysticism that does not matter. Let's move on! Like I was telling you, messages will be delivered electronically, and the new director wants to modernise the whole system. Little by little, there will be no postmen any more.' Pattabhi felt as if he had been struck by lightning. His legs shook as he gripped the edge of the table in order not to fall. The director smiled sardonically at the old postman who loved spreading wisdom. He was feeling bad for the old man and continued looking at him with one eye on the screen.

'Don't feel bad, Pattabhi, you have nothing to fear!' he said, reassuringly. 'I have already spoken to the new director who will transfer you to another department for the few years that you need to work. Three years? Four years?' He cleared his throat to get the old postman's attention. Pattabhi seemed to be living a nightmare and mumbled something.

'What did you say, Pattabhi?'

'I don't know, sir.' He was counting the number of years on his fingertips. 'Wait, I started in 1965 and now we are in… Yes, sir. That is what it is. I still have three or four years left.'

'With all the leaves that you never took, you will be left with only about one year of work,' the director added hurriedly.

Pattabhi realised at that precise moment that his last leave went back a long time ago when he had gone on a pilgrimage with his wife to Rameswaram. Apart from religious holidays, he never took leave – though the director had reminded him to do so several times. 'What will I do at home, sir? I do not know how to do anything else but deliver letters and chat with people,' was the old postman's standard reply, leaving behind him a director who adored him and had protected him all these years.

Six months later, the new director was tired and summoned the worried old postman to his office. The old pictures of Lord Ganesha and Goddess Lakshmi were replaced by an atlas which covered the whole wall. There was the latest model of computers in place of the old machine. The young director was sitting majestically in a leather chair. The old postman looked at his boss in admiration while he moved around the whole office in this chair. After a few moments of hesitation, and out of curiosity, he looked under the table and discovered that this chair had wheels! But the smell of the room had changed. The fragrance of jasmine and incense had been wiped out by a strange fragrance floating in the air.

His eyes were looking for some divine presence… a picture, a statue, something that he could pray to. There was nothing! The director was busy over the telephone and gestured towards the old postman to sit down.

'Please sit down, Pattabhi,' he said.

'Thank you, sir. I prefer standing.'

The young man sighed, looking at him. Acknowledging Pattabhi's firm stance, he did not insist.

'You see Pattabhi, in the past six months I have done everything I could to transfer you to a department from which you could retire. But there is nothing that you…'

'There is! I could be the postman once again! That is what I know how to do best!'

'Keep quiet! Don't interrupt me when I am talking,' said the director dryly. 'Who is the boss here? You or me? I have been nice to you; if it was someone else, you would already be retired, Pattabhi! Listen, I'll spare you. This is all that I can offer you, you don't have that much of a choice. It's either this or no job. It would be a pity to fire you after so many years of loyal service. I am not a heartless man. Listen to me carefully. You have only three years of service left, with a little less than one year of leave. I have spoken to my seniors;

keeping in mind bank holidays, sick leaves, etc., it would add up to three years in all. If you agree, in a week from now, you could retire. Think about it and let me know what you want in a day or two. Don't try to be clever, this is for your own good, Pattabhi.' Shattered by the news, the old postman stood there gaping. The words rang in his head like an echo of death that refused to end. He pretended to have a migraine and left work to rush to the temple close to La Poste. For the rest of the day, Ganesha, the divinity of Manakula Vinayagar, was tired of seeing the old postman in tears, crouching in the main alley of the temple.

After his bath, Pattabhiram went towards the milk booth between Rue Mission and Rue Cantine. For a change, he rushed to buy milk and go back home. He was not in a mood to talk. His wife, Visalatchi, was a little surprised to see him home so early. She made his favourite Narasu's coffee and served it on the *thinnai*. She had realised since early morning that her old husband was behaving strangely, but did not dare ask him anything, knowing that she would be talking to a wall. As much as Pattabhiram loved chatting with everyone, he spoke very little to his wife. The old postman lived in paradox: friendly towards outsiders, but a tyrant at home. Visalatchi was nothing more than a maid who had to serve her master, Pattabhiram, who took refuge in spirituality instead of enjoying conjugal bliss. The childless couple had spent half a century together in complete indifference. Visalatchi had married this strict young man without knowing that she was embarking on a long journey in an emotional desert.

She soon understood that Pattabhiram adored women more in their spiritual form than in their material form. When she shared her worries about not having children, the young man swept the problem under the carpet, embarking on a pilgrimage to different temples, letting the gods decide. Kunjithapatham, the doctor on Rue de Bussy, could have done more miracles than the entire pantheon of Hindu gods who made childbirth happen in extraordinary ways. Was not Kama the child of Lord Surya? Ayyappan was born from Vishnu, who changed into Mohini to unite with Shiva. The latter gave birth to Kartikeya by throwing his sperm in a fire that was collected by the Ganges. Visalatchi did not want any divine intervention. Just passionate love would have been enough for poor Visalatchi to have the much-awaited child. Cringing from the hurtful things people said, she accepted her unfortunate life silently.

Pattabhiram put away his bicycle in front of the Shiva temple on Mahatma Gandhi Road, much to everyone's surprise. It was a long time since they had seen the old postman in his uniform. On his last day of work, Pattabhiram was wearing his khaki shirt and pants. He was looking atrocious, his thin silhouette floating in the oversized clothes. He took off his shoes and put them away on the bicycle rack before heading for the flower and offerings shop.

'What a nice surprise to see you in a uniform, Pattabhi! Have you taken up your old job again?' asked Pajani, the shopkeeper who had known him for a long time.

'No, Pajani, unfortunately it is my last day of work.' His voice broke, his eyes filled with tears.

'Already? Aren't you happy to retire?' asked the shopkeeper, putting the jasmine garland on a coconut before handing over the offering-basket to the old man.

He paid for the basket, hesitating to talk. He would have liked to talk about his misfortune to the idol inside the temple, but the shopkeeper's inquisitive look made him speak. 'What will I do during my retirement, Pajani? My work was the only thing I knew how to do; I do not know how to do anything else. I don't have friends, family, not even a hobby! What will I do with my days?'

'You love temples. You could go on a pilgrimage with your wife.'

'Oh, my wife…' He entered the temple without finishing the conversation.

The old Raleigh steered around the traffic on Ranga Pillai Street. In spite of the trucks, carts and rickshaws blocking the way, Pattabhiram waited patiently in front of Ananda Ranga Pillai house. A small truck loaded with tomatoes blocked the road. The smell of rotten vegetables and meat filled the air.

He blocked his nose, looked to the left and stopped dreamily. Who would believe that this rundown house belonged to the most powerful man in colonial times?

This dirty, crowded and noisy street had erased the memory of the *dubash* Ananda Ranga Pillai forever. Nothing can resist eternal India. The grandeur, misery, victories and defeats, all melt to become one thin layer of dust that the collective memory is ready to blow away into oblivion. He was back on track, on his way to the temple at the crossroads of Nehru Street and Bharathi Street. He was happy! He thought about stopping for a minute to buy a garland for the director. He glanced over at the alley of florists that was in the buzzing part of the Grand Bazaar.

He looked for a place to park his bicycle. There was no place available. He walked, pushing his bicycle for a few metres. He could have parked it in front of the gate had the cows not been blocking all the parking slots. Pattabhi changed his mind. He absolutely wanted to thank his boss, who out of kindness, had given him one last day to distribute letters.

'Pattabhi, I know how sacred this job was for you. In spite of a few complaints, your career was respectable and bright. I do hope that you have understood that it is time to take retirement. The world is changing at a speed that you cannot imagine. To thank you for all these years of good service, I will let you end this spotless career where you started: the street. Moreover, I can see that you are wearing the beautiful uniform of La Poste. Go ahead, my old friend, for your last round, but come back soon. We have organised a small party for your retirement.'

Tears in his eyes, the old man shook hands with the director, thanking him profusely.

He was a little disappointed to see only a single envelope. 'Only one letter to deliver?' asked the postman, confused and embarrassed.

'*Annan*, your usual neighbourhood has been taken over by someone else. The director had insisted that I give you something. This is all I had.'

'It's all right, *Thambi*, I'll take it anyway.' He lifted the envelope with both hands solemnly. He turned it over in his hands many times and looked at it to thank God. He stopped at the address and the date. He could not understand where that was, but was intrigued by the date.

'*Thambi*, the date…'

'Yes, I know, *Annan*. This is a letter that was never delivered because nobody could find this address.'

Pattabhiram scrutinized the envelope which seemed familiar. He felt that he had already seen this name and address somewhere. The old man was known among his colleagues for his sharp memory; but in the current circumstances and in recent times he was not as confident as before. He put the letter in the left pocket of his shirt and left the office feeling confused but happy.

Pattabhiram had spent most of his day doing hardly any work. He went to meet his old clients and came back to pray in all the town temples, stopping for a break at Indian Coffee House. He was behaving like this to show to the whole town that the old postman had returned to work. After visiting the temple on Bharati Street, he went up to Nehru Street, stopping over at Singaram's who had a shop for school supplies at the corner of Rue de la Cantine. He bought new envelopes that he put away in his empty bag which looked bigger as he headed out again. 'It's high time I found this address,' he said to himself on his way back from the Muslim quarters through Mullah Street. In contrast to the Tamil quarters, this part of the town was plunged in silence.

The rare pedestrians were discreet and a few children were playing on the street in front of the houses. He went past under the confident eyes of two men who were chatting. He stopped close to the mosque and took out the envelope on which it was written: Rahamatullah Kasim, 37 Bader Sahib Street, Pondicherry 605001, South India.

'Mullah Street, the next is Cazy Street and… It must be the one afterwards.' He went straight and turned left into Milad Street, turning left again. 'Aah! Chanda Sahib Street! That's easy! You have to be stupid not to find this address!' Proud of his discovery, he counted the doors. 'Thirty-one… thirty-three… thirty-five… thirty-seven. Here it is!' He got off his bicycle and admired the beautiful blue house. It was a huge traditional Tamil house, steeped in opulence. The red Mangalore-tiled roof was in contrast with the dark blue balcony and columns, while the salmon wooden shutters made the house look even more beautiful. He parked his bicycle and rang the bell. Nobody there! He waited for a few seconds and rang the bell again. He pulled off his cap and wiped his bald head with the handkerchief around his neck. Still nobody! He gripped the bronze handle and knocked softly on the teak door.

Someone turned the handle; a young girl appeared at the doorstep.

'Yes?' she said.

'Postman,' he answered, showing her the letter.

'Postman? At this time?' Her tone was doubtful.

'Who is it for?' she asked sharply. Pattabhiram was taken aback by her rudeness. He did not like her mannerism. Who did she think she was?

'Rahamatullah Kasim!' he answered, trying to speak in the same tone.

'I don't know this person! It's not this address!' she replied dryly, irritated.

'If it is not here, where is it?' The old postman was becoming aggressive. 'Can you call someone older if you don't know?'

The young girl pretended not to hear him and grabbed the letter from Pattabhiram. She looked at the envelope and handed it back to him rudely.

'What kind of a postman are you? You do not even know how to read! It is high time you started wearing spectacles! Look, the address is Bader Sahib; this is Chanda Sahib! Learn how to read first!' The girl banged the door shut on the old postman, who stood there stunned. He was bursting with rage.

To be ill-treated by a young girl! He was angry with himself for not reading the envelope properly. He grabbed his bicycle and went to the end of the street to read the address carefully. Bader Sahib Street it said on the faded purple paper. He read it again and looked around to ask for help. 'Bader Sahib? Never heard this name before! Where the hell could it be?' he murmured. The street was deserted; he decided to return to Mullah Street where he had seen the two old men. A few minutes later, there was a small crowd around the old postman. Everyone was giving suggestions without knowing where this street was. A beggar who was rummaging in the dustbin came closer to the crowd and said, 'It is behind the Basilica of the Sacred Heart of Jesus. Take Rue Cardinal de Bausset just behind the church, then the third street on the left. You will reach Rue Latouche and Bader Sahib is on your left.'

'You are not going to trust a beggar, are you?' said one of the old men to Pattabhiram who was on the verge of leaving and said hurriedly, 'Oh, you know, beggars and postmen know the town better than anyone else!' He plonked himself on the seat thinking that it would be easier to find the street by taking Mahatma Gandhi Road, the main street. He reached the end of Mullah Street and took Rue Malquin, turning right at Ellaiamman Kovil. The sight of Ellaiamman invigorated him. It had been a long time since he came here and he tried to jog his memory. As he went closer to the temple, the memory came back. He had come here almost one year ago to deliver a letter nearby. He could not resist going into the temple and had spent a long time chatting with the priest telling him how horrified he was to discover the practices of the *devadasi*s and the devotion of the *gorappa*s at the Yellamma Temple in Saundatti.

He had lost every notion of time when he went into details about the torture rituals that the *gorappa*s adopted, as if they were dogs or horses. He was also scandalized to see almost-naked young girls parading. And like it was often the case, he postponed delivering the letter to the next day. In any case, it was a sign from the gods. He would have really wanted this letter to reach soon, but then they would not have shown him the way to the temple. There is a reason for everything, he said to himself.

He now stepped onto Tippu Sahib Street. A man was bathing in the small fountain and looked at him surprised. Pattabhiram took out the letter from his bag and looked at it. 'This is it! It is the same letter that I forgot to deliver a long time ago!' He slapped his forehead and broke into a mysterious smile. 'God wanted me to finish my work without a single mistake.' He changed his mind and moved on to Mahatma Gandhi Road heading towards the Basilica of the Sacred Heart of Jesus.

A starving red dog was lying on a rickshaw at Bader Sahib Street, looking thoroughly bored. The scorching heat and the snoring drunk rickshaw puller lying on his vehicle bench were not allowing him to take his daily nap. He looked suspiciously at the young man who was busy doing something he couldn't understand on the little piece of land between two houses. He stood up and yawned. He made a little noise because he had scraped himself with the rickshaw chain which had left a black grease stain on his face. He was in a bad mood.

A stranger stopped in front of the vacant lot. The dog would have liked to bark, but hunger stopped him from doing so when the man left. The dog was unhappy; he should have barked. A dog that doesn't bark is not a real dog, he said to himself sadly. He did not have time to be sad again as the stranger went past him. This time, the dog came out of its shelter and barked furiously. The stranger was scared and grabbed his bicycle quickly. The young man was disturbed by the barking and picked up a stone to throw at the dog, who ran away, his tail between his legs. Pattabhiram waited for a few minutes and came back to the same place. The young man was about to leave. He had finished drawing a heart with an arrow piercing through it and three drops of blood. The drawing said: 'Salim loves Suchitra.' The old postman frowned. 'Suchitra,' he said to himself. 'She is a Hindu, but he is a Muslim.' The young man stopped for a minute and stepped back to admire his masterpiece. Satisfied, he threw away the piece of coal that he was holding in his hand. The old postman approached with a smile.

'*Thambi*, please. Do you know this address? It is strange, thirty-five is there,' he said, pointing towards the yellow house. 'Thirty-nine is here… I cannot find thirty-seven. Can you please help me?' His voice was hesitant and pleading at the same time.

The young man was not in the mood to chat. He ignored the old man and started walking away without saying a word. Then, feeling a little apologetic, he came back and asked the postman.

'Who are you looking for?

'Kasim. Rahamatullah Kasim. I have to give him a letter. Do you know where he lives?' asked Pattabhiram eagerly before the young man could change his mind.

'He used to live here,' answered the young man. He turned and pointed towards the piece of land between the two houses. 'In fact, he still lives here, but we don't really know where he lives.'

'I don't understand, *Thambi*. How can anyone live in these ruins?' Pattabhiram looked confused. He looked at the land which had only three rundown walls from a house that did not exist any more. The wall on the left was just a heap of sand and bricks. Wild plants were growing inside the rooms of the house. Beer bottles and cigarette butts mingled with plastic wrappings on the dirty floor. Strangely, one room in the house was still intact.

'Kasim comes from time to time. He stays for a few days and leaves to go somewhere nobody knows. Everyone says he has lost his mind. But I am not convinced.'

'And why do people think he is crazy?' asked Pattabhiram out of curiosity. The young man burst out laughing, 'Because Kasim carries the door on his back!'

'What? I did not understand.'

'Yes, you have understood! Kasim roams around with the door of the house on his back!'

'But… why?'

'Try to find out why! Ask him yourself. And…' The young man stopped and looked at him suspiciously. 'People say he has lost his mind because of a letter.'

His colleagues were leaving when Pattabhiram returned to the post office. They looked at him accusingly. He went to the meeting room where plastic glasses, cold drinks, samosas, *bonda*s and bhajis were spread out on a table in the corner of the room.

The director's office was wide open.

'Ah! Here you are! What happened, Pattabhi? Everyone has been waiting for you since afternoon. Even on your last day of work, you have disappointed everyone.'

Wonderful! The director looked almost angry.

'I swear upon God that it was not my fault, sir!' retorted the old postman, who was regretting not having bought a garland of flowers.

'All right, if it was not your fault, I am waiting for an explanation.' Putting his elbows on the table, the director rested his chin on his hands, his right leg shaking under the table impatiently. He was finding it hard to be patient as Pattabhiram started telling his story with the minutest of details. He listened casually, playing with the paper weight which fell to the floor and rolled down near the postman's feet.

'What? You went to look for a client who roams around with a door on his back? Are you making a fool out of me, Pattabhi? It is true that I have just started my career, and I am just a novice, but please don't think I am an idiot.' The director's voice was threatening.

'No, sir! I promise you that is the truth! You can come with me and see for yourself.'

Pattabhiram had hardly finished what he was saying when the young director jumped up from his chair and shouted, 'Oh really? You want me to leave my office and go around like an ordinary postman in the town looking for a madman who goes around with a door on his back? Listen to me, this is the last warning! Do not come back to this office until you have delivered the letter! I don't care about what you are going to do! You can leave now!'

Five minutes later, after calming down, the director tried to understand the mysterious smile on the old postman's face.

Night fell gently on the town. People walking on the seaside, lazily headed home in small groups, chatting with each other, or alone, dreaming of a better tomorrow. Wandering vendors were tired at the end of the day, wearily pushing their carts back home, looking sadly at the goods that were not sold. From Nehru Street came the metallic sound of shop shutters slamming, the electric signboards switched on like dead stars in an imaginary sky. Soon, dogs would start barking to echo the sighs of miserable people looking for forbidden fruit at night. Rats would come out of gutters and run through the arteries of the town and rummage further into their night feast in cemented dustbins.

The sounds of the city died slowly to make way for the enigmatic murmurs of the night. The nocturnal face of Pondicherry is a secret meant only for lost souls like Bharat.

Lost souls like him can be found everywhere. They come out only at night, cursed to kiss its hideous face. The deserted streets become the macabre stage where shadows produce their skeletal and ephemeral music. Footpaths look like graveyards from where Pondicherry emerges, taking off its veil to embrace the dark blanket of sins. Cadavers, homeless people, unfortunates indulge in dirty pleasure in the span of the night under an ethereal sky. Vagabonds, thugs, prostitutes, beggars, thieves, drug addicts get ready to seize power in the kingdom of debauchery.

Bharat went towards the railway station. He had just left Liberty Hotel but was already thirsty. Luckily, he had carried his quota for the night. He tapped a few bottles of Old Monk tucked away in the folds of the *kaili* around his waist with satisfaction. He looked for a good place where he could hide and drink. Even though it was late, the railway station was full of life. Passengers from train number 16115 coming from Chennai Egmore poured out of the exit to take auto-rickshaws or meet those who had come to welcome them.

The place was brightly lit and full of movement. Bharat decided to go a bit further. He went his way, zig-zagging and stopped to look at the deserted Muslim quarters. Dogs barked and a beggar's voice floated in the air. Bharat opened his bottle and took a big gulp. He suddenly had a tremor. He wiped his mouth with the back of his hand, rum trickling down from his lower lip. He confidently walked towards the Basilica of the Sacred Heart of Jesus.

It had been one week since Bharat was roaming around the streets of Pondicherry. He still had not found the house. He could not remember where he lived any more. Ever since his wife had left him, he was in a drunken coma and had not returned home. He woke up at odd hours on the footpath and instinctively went to the nearest bar. He had no time to think as he fell in the treacherous arms of alcohol, roaming the streets of the entire town, having forgotten where he actually lived. But for the past two days, he would stop at the same place. Drunk and tired, some hand of destiny brought him to the same abandoned house that he had started believing belonged to him.

The rickshaw pullers' snoring enveloped the silent neighbourhood. Big rats looking for food in the middle of the street ran towards the gutter as Bharat arrived. They ran, screeching angrily, waking up the dog that was sleeping under the rickshaw. About to bark, the dog moved his ears but kept quiet. He recognised the footsteps of his new master. Since this man had come, he did not have to starve at night anymore. That was the end of roaming around the neighbourhood on an empty stomach. He no longer had to beg at the tea stall on Gandhi Road or in the Muslim quarter, where competition was tough. The newcomer spoilt him with things he had never eaten in his long and miserable life. He whimpered with joy and recognition without leaving his place. He would have loved to go and rub against the stranger. He decided not to, because he did not know what to expect. The dog remembered the last kick that had thrown him against the broken wall of the house. He just stayed there and looked over, half suspicious, half friendly.

The man stopped at the rickshaw, bent over and beckoned the dog to come closer. His hunger disappeared, giving way to an insurmountable joy. He wagged his tail frenetically. The man touched the tip of the dog's head who came out whining. Bharat and the animal went silently towards the dilapidated house. Bharat walked in the shadows towards a room that was still strangely intact. The old bedroom did not have an entrance door, but three walls were still upright.

A mat was spread along the walls on which an old, yellowed picture of Mecca was hanging. Some utensils, a trunk containing some belongings led one to believe that this otherwise spacious house was today reduced to one single room without a wall or roof. Bharat took the mat, unfolded it and sat down. He took an aluminium plate and put a packet of food on it. He had bought this meal from a street vendor on Mullah Street. There was no need to open it. The dog had already smelt the *paaya kal*. Drooling, he moved around the plate of food whining. The man was in a good mood and happily opened the newspaper packet. The dog was on the verge of devouring the first bone when a shadow stopped in front of the house. The dog looked disturbed. He looked at Bharat, then at the plate and finally at the shadow. He did not know whether he should bark, eat or pretend like nothing had happened. Bharat's inquisitive look forced him to bark. Having noticed his master's satisfied face, the dog barked even louder. A few seconds later, a stone hit him hard on the side.

'*Ading-otha!*' The rickshaw puller swore as the dog cried running away towards Gandhi Street. The man got up, murmured something inaudible and went towards the end of the street to urinate. He came back and stopped in front of the dilapidated house and looked confused.

The bells from the Basilica of the Sacred Heart of Jesus broke the heavy silence of the night. Hiding behind the smoke of the beedi, the rickshaw puller was confused: a postman, at this time of the night?

Sitting perplexed on the *thinnai*, Pattabhiram looked at the man sitting in the dilapidated room and scratched his head. This could not be Rahamatullah Kasim…

Hesitating in front of his plate, Bharat drank his rum and looked suspiciously at the newcomer. 'Who has dared to come in and sit on my *thinnai*?' grumbled the drunkard, a bit irritated.

'What! My dinner is spoilt,' added the starving dog.

While everyone observed suspiciously, another silhouette appeared at the corner of the street from nowhere. Everyone was startled to see this unusual sight: the shadow was carrying a door on its back.

Leaning on the wall with the door on his back, Rahamatullah Kasim was lost in his thoughts. The tragedy that had struck his family because of an undelivered letter had driven him insane. If this letter of acceptance from the bank had reached on time, the catastrophe would have been averted. Not being able to pay the sum of money he had received by mortgaging his house, the family was threatened by the usurer who wanted to marry his incompetent son to the daughter of the house. The bank letter was taking a long time to come. Making the best of her husband's absence, Fathima made a deadly mistake. When *datura* leaves replaced coriander, the *thalicha* became the last meal of the family. Only Rahamatullah Kasim escaped death. Having lost his head, the man left the house with the door on his back in the hope of finding the letter.

Defeated by the sequence of events, Pattabhiram did not know what to do. On the one hand, he did not know whom to give the letter to and that troubled him; on the other hand, this was a sign that the gods were postponing his retirement. Bharat, convinced that he was the master of the house who had never received any letter all his life, absolutely wanted to see this letter.

Rahamatullah Kasim did not want to get rid of the door. He did not know what to do with the letter that was lying inert on the *thinnai*.

Glossary

Advaita – school of non-dualism in Hindu philosophy, which argues against monism

Ading-otha – mother fucker

Annan – elder brother

Aiyo vellakaran! – Oh no, a white man!

Aruvamanai – a kitchen instrument with a blade

Bhogi – first day of the Tamil festival Pongal, followed by Sankranti, Mattu and Kanu

Chakravarti – a name for Lord Vishnu, one of the main gods in Hinduism, used to denote the King of the World

Charanam – end section of a Carnatic music composition, literally meaning foot

Dhavani – half-sari

Datura – poisonous plant of the nightshade Solanaceae family whose seeds and flowers, if ingested, can cause extreme discomfort or death

Dharma-shastra – a Brahmanical collection of rules of life

Dubash – interpreter

Filaos – rattan twigs

Gorappas – monks devoted to the goddess in the Yellama temple at Saundatti

Ishvara! – interjection referring to Lord Shiva

Kaal Bhairav – literally Black Shiva, the angry form of Lord Shiva, who is believed to control time

Kaili – lungi or sarong worn by men around the waist in Tamil Nadu

Kallu – toddy

Kolusu – anklets with musical bells

Kanji – congee, rice and lentil porridge

Kari Vathal – dried beef

Kepi – cap

Kolam – intricate floor decoration made with rice paste or powder

Kovil – temple

Maada kudam – altar

Maasi Magam – a festival celebrating various Hindu deities on a full moon day in the Tamil month of Maasi (February/March), coinciding with the Magam star

Manakkatai – stool

Maneki-neko – Japanese figurine

Meen Kuzhambu – fish-flavoured lentil soup with tamarind and spices

Paavadai – petticoat

Paaya kal – lamb trotters' gravy

Poonul – sacred thread worn after an initiation ceremony by upper-caste Hindu men

Perumal Kovil – temple dedicated to Lord Vishnu

Purananuru – a collection of heroic poems about kings and wars

Samkhya – dualistic school of philosophy in Hinduism based on two principles, viz., purusha or man and prakriti or nature

Saarayakadai – arrack shop

Saarayam – arrack

Sungu – hair clutch

Sundal – a savoury Tamilian snack made with chickpeas, grated coconut, mustard seeds, and curry leaves

Suprabhatam – Sanskrit morning chants sung or heard at dawn

Sura Puttu – shark fish curry

Suruttu – cheroot

Thalicha – spicy curry

Thalvaram – sloping roof

Thambi – younger brother

Tharagar – (marriage) broker

Theru Koothu – street theatre

Thinnai – porch

Thundu – piece of muslin or fine terry towelling draped over the shoulder(s) or wrapped around one's neck

Varutha Kari – fried beef

*Vellakaran*s – white men

Veshti – white or off-white sarong worn by men around the waist to cover the lower half of the body